THIS BOOK
BELONGS TO:

_____

_____

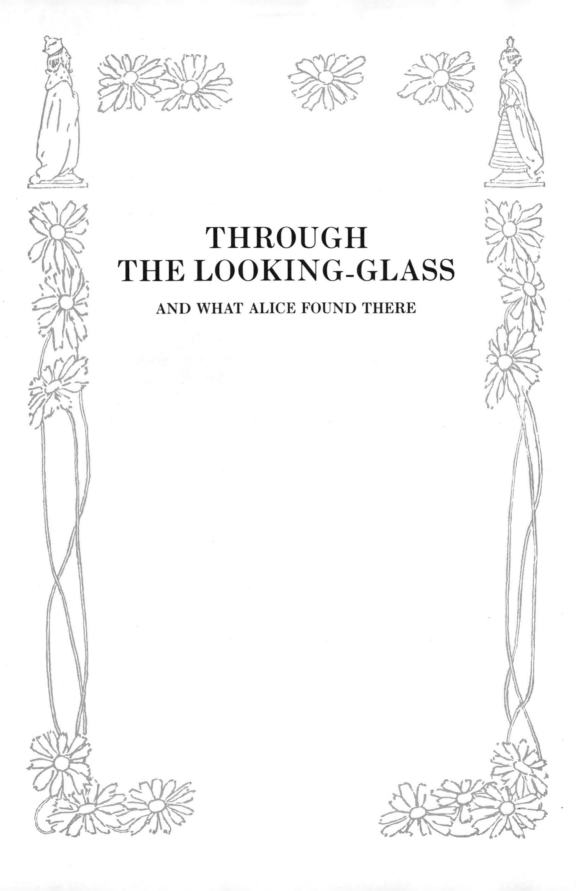

THROUGH
THE LOOKING-GLASS

AND WHAT ALICE FOUND THERE

CHILDREN'S CLASSICS

This unique series of Children's Classics™ features accessible and highly readable texts paired with the work of talented and brilliant illustrators of bygone days to create fine editions for today's parents and children to rediscover and treasure. Besides being a handsome addition to any home library, this series features genuine bonded-leather spines stamped in gold, full-color illustrations, and high-quality acid-free paper that will enable these books to be passed from one generation to the next.

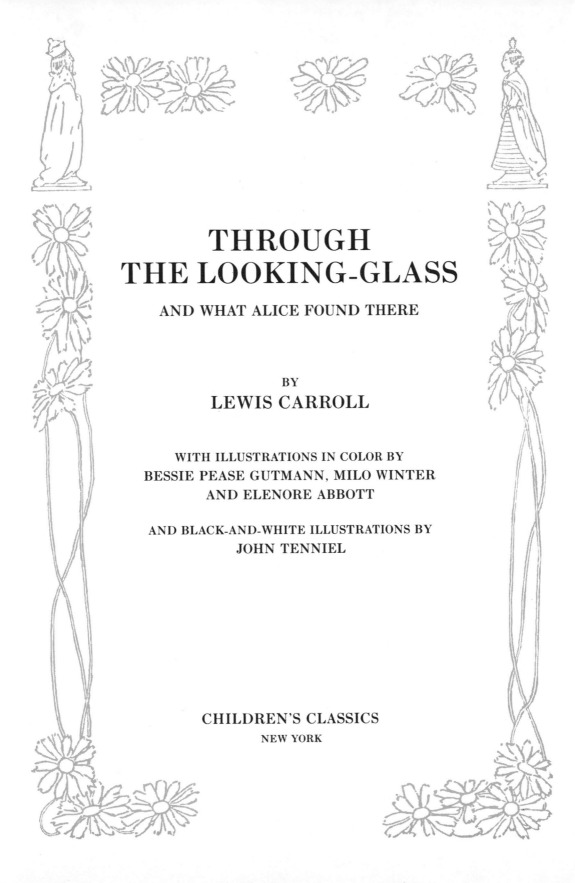

THROUGH THE LOOKING-GLASS

AND WHAT ALICE FOUND THERE

BY

LEWIS CARROLL

WITH ILLUSTRATIONS IN COLOR BY
BESSIE PEASE GUTMANN, MILO WINTER
AND ELENORE ABBOTT

AND BLACK-AND-WHITE ILLUSTRATIONS BY
JOHN TENNIEL

CHILDREN'S CLASSICS
NEW YORK

This 1990 edition is published by Children's Classics, a
division of dilithium Press, Ltd., distributed by Outlet Book
Company, Inc., a Random House Company, 225 Park Avenue
South, New York, New York 10003.

DILITHIUM is a registered trademark and CHILDREN'S
CLASSICS is a trademark of dilithium Press, Ltd.

Grateful acknowledgment is made to Macmillan, Inc. for
permission to reprint the following color illustrations by Milo
Winter: "And all the little Oysters stood" and "Humpty
Dumpty took the book". Copyright 1916, 1944 Checkerboard
Press, a division of Macmillan, Inc. All rights reserved.
Used by permission.

Printed and bound in the United States of America

Library of Congress Cataloging-in-Publication Data
Carroll, Lewis, 1832–1898.
[Through the looking-glass]
Through the looking-glass and what Alice found there /
by Lewis Carroll.
p.   cm.
Summary: In this sequel to "Alice in Wonderland," Alice goes
through the mirror to find a strange world where curious
adventures await her.
ISBN 0–517–03346–1
[1. Fantasy.]   I. Title.
PZ7.D684Th   1990
[Fic]—dc20   90–2275   CIP   AC

8   7   6   5   4   3   2   1

Cover design by Jean Krulis.

Cover illustrations by Bessie Pease Gutmann. *Front cover*:
"Now! Now!" cried the Queen. "Faster! Faster!" *(page 32)*.
Back cover: "What is it now?" said the Frog *(page 167)*.

CONTENTS

COLOR ILLUSTRATIONS

[vii]

PREFACE TO THIS ILLUSTRATED EDITION

THIS Children's Classics edition of *Through the Looking-Glass and What Alice Found There* is a cornucopia of illustration, displaying the works of four talented artists who have revealed their genius in various interpretations of Lewis Carroll's masterpiece.

John Tenniel's black-and-white drawings, which appear full-size, or enlarged, periodically throughout the text, are taken from the very first edition of the book, published in England in 1871. Although Tenniel was the first artist to illustrate this work, it was the last book of Carroll's for which he provided drawings. It contains some of his most delightfully comic portrayals.

Bessie Pease Gutmann, an American working in this country at the beginning of the century, created the majority of the color illustrations, as well as the small, occasional black-and-white spot drawings scattered throughout the text. Elenore Abbott and Milo Winter, also American painters whose golden periods were in the early decades of this century, each contributed two paintings in color. The artist for each of the color works is clearly identified on the plate.

CLAIRE BOOSS
Series Editor

1990

FOREWORD

IN *Through the Looking-Glass and What Alice Found There*, a Unicorn encounters Alice and asks,

> "What—is—this?" . . .
> "This is a child!" . . . .
> "I always thought they were fabulous monsters!" said the Unicorn . . . .

Alice replies that she had thought the same of Unicorns.

> "Well, now that we have seen each other," said the Unicorn, "if you believe in me, I'll believe in you . . ."

A bargain is also struck between the author, Lewis Carroll, and the boy or girl who reads his story. For the child who believes in Lewis Carroll finds the guideposts that Carroll left along the journey—truths of heart and mind hidden in the author's astonishing universe. The child who believes in Carroll finds that Carroll believes in him.

Lewis Carroll himself never fully grew up. To him, children were indeed "fabulous" creatures of great natural integrity, taking things at their true worth; never really convinced by adults, though often bewildered by them. When Alice steps through the looking-glass, she

[xi]

finds a world of fantastical beings—the Red Queen, the talking flowers, Humpty Dumpty, Tweedledum and Tweedledee—obeying what appear to be paradoxical rules of behavior and thought. Could these creatures—absent-minded, tyrannical, or gentle—could they be we adults?

Like many other mathematicians, Carroll seems to have longed for a perfect world, one in which the rules of the emotions would make as much sense as the laws of logic. He transformed this longing into profound comedy. The author's games of the mind lead to our questions of the heart. Thus, Humpty Dumpty tells Alice,

> "When *I* use a word, . . . it means just what I choose it to mean—neither more nor less."
> "The question is," said Alice, "whether you can make words mean so many different things."
> "The question is," said Humpty Dumpty, "which is to be master—that's all."

As Martin Gardner in *The Annotated Alice* (Bramhall House, a division of Clarkson N. Potter, New York, 1960), explains, Carroll is pointing out here that words have no inherent meaning—it is only our human minds that give them their power. By playing with language and also by reversing our notions of time and space, the author makes us wonder whether people themselves choose how they experience the world. When Alice wanders into the wood "where things have no names," she asks,

> "I wonder what will become of *my* name when I go

in? But then the fun would be, trying to find the
creature that had got my old name!.... —just
fancy calling everything you met 'Alice,' till one of
them answered."

Here, and throughout this story, Carroll playfully asks
the question, "How do we know who we are?" The
process of growing up, sometimes frightening, is a process of answering this question. Carroll takes the fears of
children and the world's other innocents seriously. In one
of the most poignant moments in the book, Alice meets a
Fawn and then walks with the animal out of the wood
"where things have no names,"

> ... here the Fawn gave a sudden bound into the air,
> and shook itself free from Alice's arm. "I'm a
> Fawn!" it cried out in a voice of delight. "And dear
> me! you're a human child!" A sudden look of alarm
> came into its beautiful brown eyes, and in another
> moment it had darted away at full speed.

We adults reading this story may be astonished by
Carroll's eccentric creatures, yet to the author it is *we*
who are the "fabulous monsters." As children delight in
identifying with the deliciously wicked witches in many
fairy tales, so Lewis Carroll identifies with the White
Queen and the Red Queen when they interrogate Alice.
Carroll, and the child who reads his book, gain control
over the villain by becoming the villain. The Red
Queen's tantrum is Carroll's tantrum,

> "I'm sure I didn't mean—" Alice was begin-

ning, but the Red Queen interrupted her impatiently.

"That's just what I complain of! You *should* have meant! What do you suppose is the use of a child without any meaning? Even a joke should have some meaning—and a child's more important than a joke, I hope. You couldn't deny that, even if you tried with both hands."

"I don't deny things with my *hands*," Alice objected.

"Nobody said you did," said the Red Queen. "I said you couldn't if you tried."

The White Queen tells Alice, "It's a poor sort of memory that only works backwards." Perhaps this is a commentary on the creative leap needed to synthesize Carroll's preoccupations as a mathematician with symbols and logic into what became his classic story—a timeless masquerade that reveals truths by disguising them. The author himself, whose real name was Charles Lutwidge Dodgson (1832–1898), was a Mathematics Lecturer at Christ Church, Oxford, but he did not express his love of the fantastical in his teaching—he was thought by most of his students to be a dull lecturer—rather, his appreciation of the absurd was manifested in his hobbies. He enjoyed inventing games and puzzles, practicing magic tricks, and attending the London theater. He first met the real Alice, Alice Liddell, in 1856, when she was almost four years old. She and her two sisters, daughters of the Dean of Christ Church, were playing in the Dean's garden as Carroll helped a friend photograph Christ

Church Cathedral from that garden. *Through the Looking Glass* (published in 1871), and the earlier *Alice's Adventures in Wonderland* (published in 1865), both stem from the tales Carroll spun for Alice and her two sisters. Indeed, throughout much of his life, Carroll made many child-friends. In the "Introduction" to *A Selection from the Letters of Lewis Carroll to His Child Friends,* (Macmillan and Co., Limited, London, 1933), the editor, Evelyn M. Hatch, describes the author,

> Mr. Dodgson was very much a part of Oxford, and those who lived there in their childhood all share the same recollections of him. Any afternoon they might meet him, in St. Giles' or the Parks—a spare erect figure, clad in the black frock-coat with loosely-tied white cravat which was the dress of the clerical don of that time. He strode along with a swift, jerky step peculiar to himself, his tall hat rather on the back of his head, and a whimsical smile hovering round his mouth.

Martin Gardner writes that the White Knight, with his "shaggy hair" and "gentle face and large mild eyes" is thought by many to be a caricature of the author. The knight, constantly falling off his horse, says, "The great art of riding...is—to keep your balance properly." The White Knight, as did Carroll, invents things,

> "What does it matter where my body happens to be? .... My mind goes on working all the same. In fact, the more head downwards I am, the more I keep inventing new things."

[xv]

FOREWORD

This book is not an easy book. By intriguing the child's mind, it engages his heart. One might say *Through the Looking-Glass* is a child's *Don Quixote*. We feel that Carroll's uncompromising characters, involved in their puzzling adventures, share the resonance of dreams—they disconcert, they startle—but at the end of our journey *Through the Looking-Glass*, we find, with Alice, that we have faced our fears and survived. In many re-readings of this story throughout our lives, we shall be searching for the keys to this perplexing tale. Perhaps the finest thing that can be said of *Through the Looking-Glass* should be left to Alice,

"It's exactly like a riddle with no answer!"

ELLEN S. SHAPIRO

Brooklyn, New York
1990

[xvi]

AUTHOR'S PREFACE

AS the chess-problem, given on the following page, has puzzled some of my readers, it may be well to explain that it is correctly worked out, so far as the *moves* are concerned. The *alternation* of Red and White is perhaps not so strictly observed as it might be, and the "castling" of the three Queens is merely a way of saying that they entered the palace: but the "check" of the White King at move 6, the capture of the Red Knight at move 7, and the final "checkmate" of the Red King, will be found, by any one who will take the trouble to set the pieces and play the moves as directed, to be strictly in accordance with the laws of the game.

The new words, in the poem "Jabberwocky" (see p. 17), have given rise to some differences of opinion as to their pronunciation: so it may be well to given instructions on *that* point also. Pronounce "slithy" as if it were the two words "sly, the": make the 'g' *hard* in "gyre" and "gimble": and pronounce "rath" to rhyme with "bath."

White Pawn (Alice) to play, and win in eleven moves.

INTRODUCTION

CHILD of the pure unclouded brow
  And dreaming eyes of wonder!
Though time be fleet, and I and thou
  Are half a life asunder,
Thy loving smile will surely hail
The love-gift of a fairy-tale.

I have not seen thy sunny face,
  Nor heard thy silver laughter:
No thought of me shall find a place
  In thy young life's hereafter—
Enough that now thou wilt not fail
To listen to my fairy-tale.

A tale begun in other days,
  When summer suns were glowing—
A simple chime, that served to time
  The rhythm of our rowing—
Whose echoes live in memory yet,
'Though envious years would say 'forget.'

Come, hearken then, ere voice of dread,
  With bitter tidings laden,
Shall summon to unwelcome bed
  A melancholy maiden!
We are but older children, dear,
Who fret to find our bedtime near.

[xix]

INTRODUCTION

Without, the frost, the blinding snow,
   The storm-wind's moody madness—
Within, the firelight's ruddy glow,
   And childhood's nest of gladness.
The magic words shall hold thee fast:
Thou shalt not heed the raving blast.

And, though the shadow of a sigh
   May tremble through the story,
For 'happy summer days,' gone by,
   And vanish'd summer glory—
It shall not touch, with breath of bale,
The pleasance of our fairy-tale.

LOOKING-GLASS HOUSE

ONE thing was certain, that the *white* kitten had had nothing to do with it —it was the black kitten's fault entirely. For the white kitten had been having its face washed by the old cat for the last quarter of an hour (and bearing it pretty well, considering): so you see that it *couldn't* have had any hand in the mischief.

The way Dinah washed her children's faces was this: first she held the poor thing down by its ear with one paw, and then with the other paw she rubbed its face all over, the wrong way, beginning at the nose: and just now, as I said, she was hard at work on the white kitten, which was lying quite still and trying to purr—no doubt feeling that it was all meant for its good.

But the black kitten had been finished with

 THROUGH THE

earlier in the afternoon, and so, while Alice was sitting curled up in a corner of the great arm-chair, half talking to herself and half asleep, the kitten had been having a grand game of romps with the ball of worsted Alice had been trying to wind up, and had been rolling it up and down till it had all come undone again; and there it was, spread over the hearth-rug, all knots and tangles, with the kitten running after its own tail in the middle.

"Oh, you wicked wicked little thing!" cried Alice, catching up the kitten, and giving it a little kiss to make it understand that it was in disgrace. "Really, Dinah ought to have taught you better manners! You *ought,* Dinah, you know you ought!" she added, looking reproachfully at the old cat, and speaking in as cross a voice as she could manage—and then she

  LOOKING GLASS

scrambled back into the arm-chair, taking the kitten and the worsted with her, and began winding up the ball again. But she didn't get on very fast, as she was talking all the time, sometimes to the kitten, and sometimes to herself. Kitty sat very demurely on her knee, pretending to watch the progress of the winding, and now and then putting out one paw and gently touching the ball, as if it would be glad to help if it might.

"Do you know what to-morrow is, Kitty?" Alice began. "You'd have guessed if you'd been up in the window with me—only Dinah was making you tidy, so you couldn't. I was watching the boys getting in sticks for the bonfire—and it wants plenty of sticks, Kitty! Only it got so cold, and it snowed so, they had to leave off. Never mind, Kitty, we'll go and see the bonfire to-morrow." Here Alice wound two or three turns of the worsted round the kitten's neck, just to see how it would look: this led to a scramble, in which the ball rolled down upon the floor, and yards and yards of it got unwound again.

[3]

 # THROUGH THE

"Do you know, I was so angry, Kitty,"
Alice went on, as soon as they were comfortably settled again, "when I saw all the mischief you had been doing, I was very nearly
opening the window, and putting you out into
the snow! And you'd have deserved it, you
little mischievous darling! What have you
got to say for yourself? Now don't interrupt
me!" she went on, holding up one finger. "I'm
going to tell you all your faults. Number one:
you squeaked twice while Dinah was washing
your face this morning. Now you can't deny
it, Kitty: I heard you! What's that you say?"
(pretending that the kitten was speaking).
"Her paw went into your eye? Well, that's
your fault, for keeping your eyes open—if
you'd shut them tight up, it wouldn't have happened. Now don't make any more excuses,
but listen! Number two: you pulled Snowdrop away by the tail just as I had put down
the saucer of milk before her! What, you were
thirsty, were you? How do you know she
wasn't thirsty too? Now for number three:

[4]

you unwound every bit of the worsted while I wasn't looking!

"That's three faults, Kitty, and you've not been punished for any of them yet. You know I'm saving up all your punishments for Wednesday week—Suppose they had saved up all *my* punishments?" she went on, talking more to herself than the kitten. "What *would* they do at the end of a year? I should be sent to prison, I suppose, when the day came. Or —let me see—suppose each punishment was to be going without a dinner: then, when the miserable day came, I should have to go without fifty dinners at once! Well, I shouldn't mind *that* much! I'd far rather go without them than eat them!

"Do you hear the snow against the window-panes, Kitty? How nice and soft it sounds! Just as if some one was kissing the window all over outside. I wonder if the snow *loves* the trees and fields, that it kisses them so gently? And then it covers them up snug, you know, with a white quilt; and perhaps it says 'Go to

[5]

sleep, darlings, till the summer comes again.' And when they wake up in the summer, Kitty, they dress themselves all in green, and dance about—whenever the wind blows—oh, that's very pretty!" cried Alice, dropping the ball of worsted to clap her hands. "And I do so *wish* it was true! I'm sure the woods look sleepy in the autumn, when the leaves are getting brown.

"Kitty, can you play chess? Now, don't smile, my dear, I'm asking it seriously. Because, when we were playing just now, you watched just as if you understood it: and when I said 'Check!' you purred! Well, it *was* a nice check, Kitty, and really I might have won, if it hadn't been for that nasty Knight, that came wriggling down among my pieces. Kitty, dear, let's pretend—" And here I wish I could tell you half the things Alice used to say, beginning with her favourite phrase "Let's pretend." She had had quite a long argument with her sister only the day before—all because Alice had begun with "Let's pretend we're

LOOKING GLASS

kings and queens;" and her sister, who liked
being very exact, had argued that they
couldn't, because there were only two of them,
and Alice had been reduced at last to say
"Well, *you* can be one of them, then, and *I'll*
be all the rest." And once she had really
frightened her old nurse by shouting suddenly in her ear, "Nurse! Do let's pretend
that I'm a hungry hyæna, and you're a
bone!"

But this is taking us away from Alice's
speech to the kitten. "Let's pretend that
you're the Red Queen, Kitty! Do you know,
I think if you sat up and folded your arms,
you'd look exactly like her. Now do try,
there's a dear!" And Alice got the Red Queen
off the table, and set it up before the kitten as
a model for it to imitate: however, the thing
didn't succeed, principally, Alice said, because
the kitten wouldn't fold its arms properly. So,
to punish it, she held it up to the Looking-
glass, that it might see how sulky it was, "—
and if you're not good directly," she added,

[7]

# THROUGH THE

"I'll put you through into Looking-glass House. How would you like *that?*

"Now, if you'll only attend, Kitty, and not talk so much, I'll tell you all my ideas about Looking-glass House. First, there's the room you can see through the glass—that's just the same as our drawing-room, only the things go the other way. I can see all of it when I get upon a chair—all but the bit just behind the fireplace. Oh! I do so wish I could see *that* bit! I want so much to know whether they've a fire in the winter: you never *can* tell, you know, unless our fire smokes, and then smoke comes up in that room too—but that may be only pretence, just to make it look as if they had a fire. Well then, the books are something like our books, only the words go the wrong way: I know *that,* because I've held up one of our books to the glass, and then they hold up one in the other room.

"How would you like to live in Looking-glass House, Kitty? I wonder if they'd give you milk in there? Perhaps Looking-glass

# LOOKING GLASS

milk isn't good to drink—but oh, Kitty! now we come to the passage. You can just see a little *peep* of the passage in Looking-glass House, if you leave the door of our drawing-room wide open: and it's very like our passage as far as you can see, only you know it may be quite different on beyond. Oh, Kitty, how nice it would be if we could only get through into Looking-glass House! I'm sure it's got, oh! such beautiful things in it! Let's pretend there's a way of getting through into it, some-how, Kitty. Let's pretend the glass has got all soft like gauze, so that we can get through. Why, it's turning into a sort of mist now, I declare! It'll be easy enough to get through—" She was up on the chimney-piece while she said this, though she hardly knew how she had got there. And certainly the glass *was* begin-ning to melt away, just like a bright silvery mist.

In another moment Alice was through the glass, and had jumped lightly down into the Looking-glass room. The very first thing she

did was to look whether there was a fire in the
fireplace, and she was quite pleased to find that
there was a real one, blazing away as brightly
as the one she had left behind. "So I shall be
as warm here as I was in the old room,"
thought Alice: "warmer, in fact, because
there'll be no one here to scold me away from
the fire. Oh, what fun it'll be, when they see
me through the glass in here, and can't get
at me!"

Then she began looking about, and noticed
that what could be seen from the old room was
quite common and uninteresting, but that all
the rest was as different as possible. For instance, the pictures on the wall next the fire
seemed to be all alive, and the very clock on the
chimney-piece (you know you can only see the
back of it in the Looking-glass) had got the
face of a little old man, and grinned at her.

"They don't keep this room so tidy as the
other," Alice thought to herself, as she noticed
several of the chessmen down in the hearth
among the cinders; but in another moment,

Certainly the glass *was* beginning to melt away.

Page 9

In another moment, Alice was through the glass.

Page 9

LKING GLASS

with a little "Oh!" of surprise, she was down on her hands and knees watching them. The chessmen were walking about, two and two!

"Here are the Red King and the Red Queen," Alice said (in a whisper, for fear of frightening them), "and there are the White King and the White Queen sitting on the edge of the shovel—and here are two Castles walking arm in arm—I don't think they can hear me," she went on, as she put her head closer down, "and I'm nearly sure they can't see me. I feel somehow as if I was getting invisible——"

Here something began squeaking on the table behind Alice, and made her turn her head just in time to see one of the White Pawns roll over and begin kicking: she watched it with great curiosity to see what would happen next.

"It is the voice of my child!" the White Queen cried out, as she rushed past the King, so violently that she knocked him over among the cinders. "My precious Lily! My imperial

[11]

kitten!" and she began scrambling wildly up the side of the fender.

"Imperial fiddlestick!" said the King, rubbing his nose, which had been hurt by the fall. He had a right to be a *little* annoyed with the Queen, for he was covered with ashes from head to foot.

Alice was very anxious to be of use, and, as the poor little Lily was nearly screaming herself into a fit, she hastily picked up the Queen and set her on the table by the side of her noisy little daughter.

The Queen gasped, and sat down; the rapid journey through the air had quite taken away her breath, and for a minute or two she could do nothing but hug the little Lily in silence. As soon as she had recovered her breath a little, she called out to the White King, who was sitting sulkily among the ashes, "Mind the volcano!"

"What volcano?" said the King, looking up anxiously into the fire, as if he thought that was the most likely place to find one.

[12]

LOOKING GLASS

"Blew—me—up," panted the Queen, who was still a little out of breath. "Mind you come up—the regular way—don't get blown up!"

Alice watched the White King as he slowly struggled up from bar to bar, till at last she said, "Why, you'll be hours and hours getting to the table, at that rate. I'd far better help you, hadn't I?" But the King took no notice of the question: it was quite clear that he could neither hear her nor see her.

So Alice picked him up very gently, and lifted him across more slowly than she had lifted the Queen, that she mightn't take his breath away; but, before she put him on the table, she thought she might as well dust him a little, he was so covered with ashes.

She said afterwards that she had never seen in all her life such a face as the King made, when he found himself held in the air by an invisible hand, and being dusted: he was far too much astonished to cry out, but his eyes and his mouth went on getting larger and larger, and rounder and rounder, till her hand shook

y

so with laughing that she nearly let him drop upon the floor.

"Oh! *please* don't make such faces, my dear!" she cried out, quite forgetting that the King couldn't hear her. "You make me laugh so that I can hardly hold you! And don't keep your mouth so wide open! All the ashes will get into it—there, now I think you're tidy enough!" she added, as she smoothed his hair, and set him upon the table near the Queen.

The King immediately fell flat on his back, and lay perfectly still; and Alice was a little alarmed at what she had done, and went round the room to see if she could find any water to throw over him. However, she could find nothing but a bottle of ink, and when she got back with it she found he had recovered, and he and the Queen were talking together in a frightened whisper—so low that Alice could hardly hear what they said.

The King was saying, "I assure you, my dear, I turned cold to the very ends of my whiskers!"

[14]

LOOKING GLASS

To which the Queen replied, "You haven't got any whiskers."

"The horror of that moment," the King went on, "I shall never, *never* forget!"

"You will, though," the Queen said, "if you don't make a memorandum of it."

Alice looked on with great interest as the King took an enormous memorandum-book out of his pocket and began writing. A sudden thought struck her, and she took hold of the end of the pencil, which came some way over his shoulder, and began writing for him.

The poor King looked puzzled and unhappy, and struggled with the pencil for some time without saying anything; but Alice was too strong for him, and at last he panted out, "My dear! I really *must* get a thinner pencil. I can't manage this one a bit; it writes all manner of things that I don't intend——"

"What manner of things?" said the Queen, looking over the book

 # THROUGH THE

(in which Alice had put *"The White Knight is sliding down the poker. He balances very badly."*) "That's not a memorandum of *your* feelings!"

There was a book lying near Alice on the table, and while she sat watching the White King (for she was still a little anxious about him, and had the ink all ready to throw over him in case he fainted again), she turned over the leaves to find some part that she could read, "For it's all in some language I don't know," she said to herself.

It was like this:

JABBERWOCKY

'Twas brillig, and the slithy toves
Did gyre and gimble in the wabe:
All mimsy were the borogoves,
And the mome raths outgrabe.

She puzzled over this for some time, but at last a bright thought struck her. "Why, it's a Looking-glass book, of course! And if

[16]

LOOKING GLASS

I hold it up to a glass the words will all go the right way again."

This was the poem that Alice read:

JABBERWOCKY

'Twas brillig, and the slithy toves
Did gyre and gimble in the wabe:
All mimsy were the borogoves,
And the mome raths outgrabe.

"Beware the Jabberwock, my son!
The jaws that bite, the claws that catch!
Beware the Jubjub bird, and shun
The frumious Bandersnatch!"

He took his vorpal sword in hand:
Long time the manxome foe he sought—
So rested he by the Tumtum tree,
And stood awhile in thought.

And, as in uffish thought he stood,
The Jabberwock, with eyes of flame,
Came whiffling through the tulgey wood,
And burbled as it came!

[17]

THROUGH THE

One, two! One, two! And through and through
The vorpal blade went snicker-snack!
He left it dead, and with its head
He went galumphing back.

"And hast thou slain the Jabberwock?
Come to my arms, my beamish boy!
O frabjous day! Callooh! Callay!"
He chortled in his joy.

'Twas brillig, and the slithy toves
Did gyre and gimble in the wabe:
All mimsy were the borogoves,
And the mome raths outgrabe

"It seems very pretty," she said when she had finished it, "but it's *rather* hard to understand!" (You see she didn't like to confess, even to herself, that she couldn't make it out at all.) "Somehow it seems to fill my head with ideas—only I don't exactly know what they are! However, *somebody* killed *something;* that's clear, at any rate——"

"But oh!" thought Alice, suddenly jumping up, "if I don't make haste I shall have to go

[18]

The chessmen were walking about, two and two!

Page 11

The Jabberwock with eyes of flame,
Came whiffling through the tulgey wood.

Page 17

LOOKING GLASS

back through the Looking-glass before I've
seen what the rest of the house is like! Let's
have a look at the garden first!" She was out
of the room in a moment, and ran downstairs
—or, at least, it wasn't exactly running, but a
new invention for getting downstairs quickly
and easily, as Alice said to herself. She just
kept the tips of her fingers on the hand-rail and
floated gently down without even touching the
stairs with her feet; then she floated on through
the hall, and would have gone straight out at
the door in the same way if she hadn't caught
hold of the door-post. She was getting a little
giddy with so much floating in the air, and was
rather glad to find herself walking again in the
natural way.

THROUGH THE

THE GARDEN OF LIVE FLOWERS

"I SHOULD see the garden far better," said Alice to herself, "if I could get to the top of that hill; and here's a path that leads straight to it—at least, no, it doesn't do *that*—" (after going a few yards along the path, and turning several sharp corners), "but I suppose it will at last. But how curiously it twists! It's more like a corkscrew than a path! Well, *this* turn goes to the hill, I suppose—no, it doesn't! This goes straight back to the house! Well, then, I'll try it the other way."

And so she did, wandering up and down and trying turn after turn, but always coming back to the house, do what she would. Indeed, once, when she had turned a corner rather more quickly than usual, she ran against it before she could stop herself.

"It's no use talking about it," Alice said,

LOOKING GLASS

looking up at the house and pretending it was arguing with her. "I'm *not* going in again yet. I know I should have to get through the Looking-glass again—back into the old room —and there'd be an end of all my adventures!"

So, resolutely turning her back upon the house, she set out once more down the path, determined to keep straight on till she got to the hill. For a few minutes all went on well, and she was just saying, "I really *shall* do it this time—" when the path gave a sudden twist and shook itself (as she described it afterwards), and the next moment she found herself actually walking in at the door.

"Oh, it's too bad!" she cried. "I never saw such a house for getting in the way! Never!"

However, there was the hill in full sight, so there was nothing to be done but start again. This time she came upon a large flower-bed, with a border of daisies, and a willow-tree growing in the middle.

"O Tiger-lily!" said Alice, addressing her-

[21]

self to one that was waving gracefully about in the wind, "I *wish* you could talk!"

"We *can* talk," said the Tiger-lily, "when there's anybody worth talking to."

Alice was so astonished that she couldn't speak for a minute: it quite seemed to take her breath away. At length, as the Tiger-lily only went on waving about, she spoke again, in a timid voice—almost in a whisper. "And can *all* the flowers talk?"

"As well as *you* can," said the Tiger-lily. "And a great deal louder."

"It isn't manners for us to begin, you know," said the Rose, "and I really was wondering when you'd speak! Said I to myself, 'Her face has got *some* sense in it, though it's not a clever one!' Still, you're the right color, and that goes a long way."

"I don't care about the color," the Tiger-lily remarked. "If only her petals curled up a little more, she'd be all right."

Alice didn't like being criticized, so she began asking questions. "Aren't you sometimes

[22]

frightened at being planted out here, with no-body to take care of you?"

"There's the tree in the middle," said the Rose. "What else is it good for?"

"But what could it do if any danger came?" Alice asked.

"It could bark," said the Rose.

"It says, 'Bough-wough!'" cried a Daisy. "That's why its branches are called boughs!"

"Didn't you know *that?*" cried another Daisy. And here they all began shouting together, till the air seemed quite full of little shrill voices. "Silence, every one of you!" cried the Tiger-lily, waving itself passionately from side to side and trembling with excitement. "They know I can't get at them!" it panted, bending its quivering head towards Alice, "or they wouldn't dare to do it!"

"Never mind!" Alice said in a soothing tone,

[23]

and, stooping down to the daisies, who were just beginning again, she whispered, "If you don't hold your tongues I'll pick you!"

There was silence in a moment, and several of the pink daisies turned white.

"That's right!" said the Tiger-lily. "The Daisies are worst of all. When one speaks, they all begin together, and it's enough to make one wither to hear the way they go on!"

"How is it you can all talk so nicely?" Alice said, hoping to get it into a better temper by a compliment. "I've been in many gardens before, but none of the flowers could talk."

"Put your hand down and feel the ground," said the Tiger-lily. "Then you'll know why."

Alice did so. "It's very hard," she said; "but I don't see what that has to do with it."

"In most gardens," the Tiger-lily said, "they make the beds too soft—so that the flowers are always asleep."

This sounded a very good reason, and Alice was quite pleased to know it. "I never thought of that before!" she said.

[24]

"It's *my* opinion that you never think *at all*," the Rose said, in a rather severe tone.

"I never saw anybody that looked stupider," a Violet said so suddenly that Alice quite jumped, for it hadn't spoken before.

"Hold *your* tongue!" cried the Tiger-lily. "As if *you* ever saw anybody! You keep your head under the leaves, and snore away there till you know no more what's going on in the world than if you were a bud!"

"Are there any more people in the garden besides me?" Alice said, not choosing to notice the Rose's last remark.

"There's one other flower in the garden that can move about like you," said the Rose. "I wonder how you do it—" ("You're always wondering," said the Tiger-lily), "but she's more bushy than you are."

"Is she like me?" Alice asked eagerly, for the thought crossed her mind, "There's another little girl in the garden somewhere!"

"Well, she has the same awkward shape as

[25]

you," the Rose said; "but she's redder—and her petals are shorter, I think."

"They're done up close, like a Dahlia," said the Tiger-lily; "not tumbled about like yours."

"But that's not *your* fault," the Rose added kindly. "You're beginning to fade, you know—and then one can't help one's petals getting a little untidy."

Alice didn't like this idea at all; so, to change the subject, she asked, "Does she ever come out here?"

"I daresay you'll see her soon," said the Rose. "She's one of the kind that has nine spikes, you know."

"Where does she wear them?" Alice asked with some curiosity.

"Why, all round her head, of course," the Rose replied. "I was wondering *you* hadn't got some, too. I thought it was the regular rule."

"She's coming!" cried the Larkspur. "I hear her footstep, thump, thump, along the gravel-walk!"

Alice looked round eagerly and found that

LOOKING GLASS

it was the Red Queen. "She's grown a good deal!" was her first remark. She had indeed: when Alice first found her in the ashes she had been only three inches high—and here she was half a head taller than Alice herself!

"It's the fresh air that does it," said the Rose; "wonderfully fine air it is out here."

"I think I'll go and meet her," said Alice, for though the flowers were interesting enough, she felt that it would be far grander to have a talk with a real Queen.

"You can't possibly do that," said the Rose. "*I* should advise you to walk the other way."

This sounded nonsense to Alice, so she said nothing, but set off at once towards the Red Queen. To her surprise she lost sight of her in a moment, and found herself walking in at the front door again.

A little provoked, she drew back, and after looking everywhere for the Queen (whom she spied out at last, a long way off) she thought she would try the plan this time of walking in the opposite direction.

[27]

 # THROUGH THE

It succeeded beautifully. She had not been walking a minute before she found herself face to face with the Red Queen, and full in sight of the hill she had been so long aiming at.

"Where do you come from?" said the Red Queen. "And where are you going? Look up, speak nicely, and don't twiddle your fingers all the time."

Alice attended to all these directions, and explained, as well as she could, that she had lost her way.

"I don't know what you mean by *your* way," said the Queen; "all the ways about here belong to *me*—but why did you come out here at all?" she added in a kinder tone. "Curtsey while you're thinking what to say. It saves time."

Alice wondered a little at this, but she was too much in awe of the Queen to disbelieve it. "I'll try it when I go home," she thought to herself, "the next time I'm a little late for dinner."

"It's time for you to answer now," the Queen said, looking at her watch; "open your mouth

LꝎKING GLASS

a *little* wider when you speak, and always say 'your Majesty.'"

"I only wanted to see what the garden was like, your Majesty——"

"That's right," said the Queen, patting her on the head, which Alice didn't like at all; "though when you say 'garden'—*I've* seen gardens compared with which this would be a wilderness."

Alice didn't dare to argue the point, but went on: "—and I thought I'd try and find my way to the top of that hill——"

"When you say 'hill,'" the Queen interrupted, "*I* could show you hills in comparison with which you'd call that a valley."

"No, I shouldn't," said Alice, surprised into contradicting her at last; "a hill *can't* be a valley, you know. That would be nonsense——"

The Red Queen shook her head. "You may call it 'nonsense' if you like," she said, "but *I've* heard nonsense compared with which that would be as sensible as a dictionary!"

THROUGH THE

Alice curtseyed again, as she was afraid from the Queen's tone that she was a *little* offended, and they walked on in silence till they got to the top of the little hill.

For some minutes Alice stood without speaking, looking out in all directions over the country—and a most curious country it was. There were a number of tiny little brooks running straight across it from side to side, and the ground between was divided up into squares by a number of little green hedges, that reached from brook to brook.

"I declare, it's marked out just like a large chess-board!" Alice said at last. "There ought to be some men moving about somewhere—and so there are!" she added in a tone of delight, and her heart began to beat quick with excitement as she went on. "It's a great, huge game of chess that's being played—all over the world—if this *is* the world at all, you know. Oh, what fun it is! How I *wish* I was one of them! I wouldn't mind being a Pawn, if only

# LOOKING GLASS

I might join—though of course I should *like* to be a Queen best."

She glanced rather shyly at the real Queen as she said this, but her companion only smiled pleasantly, and said, "That's easily managed. You can be the White Queen's Pawn, if you like, as Lily's too young to play; and you're in the Second Square to begin with. When you get to the Eighth Square you'll be a Queen—" Just at this moment, somehow or other, they began to run.

Alice never could quite make out, in thinking it over afterwards, how it was that they began; all she remembers is, that they were running hand in hand, and the Queen went so fast that it was all she could do to keep up with her; and still the Queen kept crying, "Faster! Faster!" but Alice felt she *could not* go faster, though she had no breath left to say so.

The most curious part of the thing was, that the trees and the other things round them never changed their places at all: however fast they went, they never seemed to pass anything. "I

wonder if all the things move along with us?" thought poor puzzled Alice. And the Queen seemed to guess her thoughts, for she cried, "Faster! Don't try to talk!"

Not that Alice had any idea of doing *that*. She felt as if she would never be able to talk again, she was getting so much out of breath: and still the Queen cried, "Faster! Faster!" and dragged her along. "Are we nearly there?" Alice managed to pant out at last.

"Nearly there!" the Queen repeated. "Why, we passed it ten minutes ago! Faster!" And they ran on for a time in silence, with the wind whistling in Alice's ears, and almost blowing her hair off her head, she fancied.

"Now! Now!" cried the Queen. "Faster! Faster!" And they went so fast that at last they seemed to skim through the air, hardly touching the ground with their feet, till suddenly, just as Alice was getting quite exhausted, they stopped, and she found herself sitting on the ground, breathless and giddy.

The Queen propped her up against a tree,

and said kindly, "You may rest a little now."

Alice looked round her in great surprise. "Why, I do believe we've been under this tree the whole time! Everything's just as it was!"

"Of course it is," said the Queen. "What would you have it?"

"Well, in *our* country," said Alice, still panting a little, "you'd generally get to somewhere else—if you ran very fast for a long time as we've been doing."

"A slow sort of country!" said the Queen. "Now *here,* you see, it takes all the running *you* can do to keep in the same place. If you want to get somewhere else, you must run at least twice as fast as that!"

"I'd rather not try, please!" said Alice. "I'm quite content to stay here—only I *am* so hot and thirsty!"

"I know what *you'd* like!" the Queen said good-naturedly, taking a little box out of her pocket. "Have a biscuit?"

Alice thought it would not be civil to say

[33]

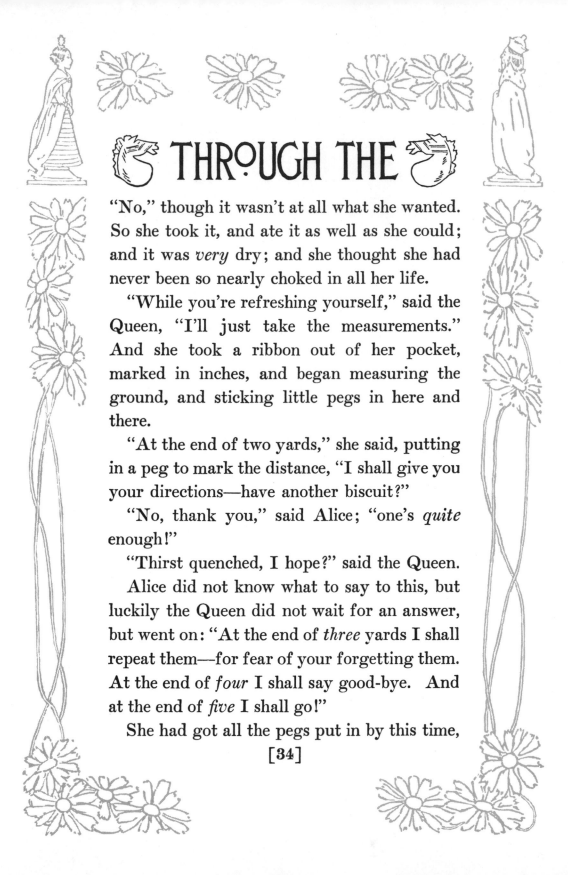

"No," though it wasn't at all what she wanted. So she took it, and ate it as well as she could; and it was *very* dry; and she thought she had never been so nearly choked in all her life.

"While you're refreshing yourself," said the Queen, "I'll just take the measurements." And she took a ribbon out of her pocket, marked in inches, and began measuring the ground, and sticking little pegs in here and there.

"At the end of two yards," she said, putting in a peg to mark the distance, "I shall give you your directions—have another biscuit?"

"No, thank you," said Alice; "one's *quite* enough!"

"Thirst quenched, I hope?" said the Queen.

Alice did not know what to say to this, but luckily the Queen did not wait for an answer, but went on: "At the end of *three* yards I shall repeat them—for fear of your forgetting them. At the end of *four* I shall say good-bye. And at the end of *five* I shall go!"

She had got all the pegs put in by this time,

and Alice looked on with great interest as she returned to the tree, and then began slowly walking down the row.

At the two-yard peg she faced round, and said, "A pawn goes two squares in its first move, you know. So you'll go *very* quickly through the Third Square—by railway, I should think—and you'll find yourself in the Fourth Square in no time. Well, *that* square belongs to Tweedledum and Tweedledee—the Fifth is mostly water—the Sixth belongs to Humpty Dumpty—But you make no remark?"

"I—I didn't know I had to make one—just then," Alice faltered out.

"You *should* have said," the Queen went on in a tone of grave reproof, " 'It's extremely kind of you to tell me all this'—however, we'll suppose it said—the Seventh Square is all forest—however, one of the Knights will show you the way—and in the Eighth Square we shall be Queens together, and it's all feasting and fun!" Alice got up and curtseyed and sat down again.

At the next peg the Queen turned again, and this time she said, "Speak in French when you can't think of the English for a thing—turn out your toes as you walk—and remember who you are!" She did not wait for Alice to curtsey this time, but walked on quickly to the next peg, where she turned for a moment to say "Good-bye," and then hurried on to the last.

How it happened Alice never knew, but exactly as she came to the last peg she was gone. Whether she vanished into the air or whether she ran quickly into the wood ("and she *can* run very fast!" thought Alice), there was no way of guessing, but she was gone, and Alice began to remember that she was a Pawn, and that it would soon be time for her to move.

LOOKING-GLASS INSECTS

O F course the first thing to do was to make a grand survey of the country she was going to travel through. "It's something very like learning geography," thought Alice, as she stood on tiptoe in hopes of being able to see a little further. "Princi-pal rivers—there *are* none. Principal moun-tains—I'm on the only one, but I don't think it's got any name. Principal towns—why, what *are* those creatures, making honey down there? They can't be bees—nobody ever saw bees a mile off, you know—" and for some time she stood silent, watching one of them that was bustling about among the flowers, poking its proboscis into them, "just as if it was a regular bee," thought Alice.

However, this was anything but a regular bee; in fact, it was an elephant—as Alice soon

[37]

THROUGH THE

found out, though the idea quite took her breath away at first. "And what enormous flowers they must be!" was her next idea. "Something like cottages with the roofs taken off, and stalks put to them—and what quantities of honey they must make! I think I'll go down and—no, I won't go *just* yet," she went on, checking herself just as she was beginning to run down the hill, and trying to find some excuse for turning shy so suddenly. "It'll never do to go down among them without a good long branch to brush them away— and what fun it'll be when they ask me how I liked my walk. I shall say, 'Oh, I liked it well enough—' (here came the favourite little toss of the head), 'only it *was* so dusty and hot, and the elephants *did* tease so!'

"I think I'll go down the other way," she said after a pause; "and perhaps I may visit the elephants later on. Besides, I *do* so want to get into the Third Square!"

So, with this excuse, she ran down the hill

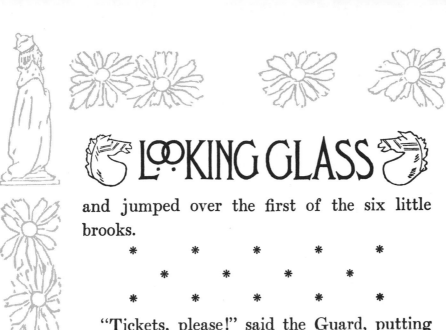

LOOKING GLASS

and jumped over the first of the six little brooks.

*　　*　　*　　*　　*

　*　　*　　*　　*

　*　　*　　*　　*　　*

"Tickets, please!" said the Guard, putting his head in at the window. In a moment everybody was holding out a ticket: they were about the same size as the people, and quite seemed to fill the carriage.

"Now, then! Show your ticket, child!" the Guard went on, looking angrily at Alice. And a great many voices all said together ("like the chorus of a song," thought Alice), "Don't keep him waiting, child! Why, his time is worth a thousand pounds a minute!"

"I'm afraid I haven't got one," Alice said in a frightened tone; "there wasn't a ticket-office where I came from." And again the chorus of voices went on. "There wasn't room for one where she came from. The land there is worth a thousand pounds an inch!"

"Don't make excuses," said the Guard; "you

THROUGH THE

should have bought one from the engine-driver." And once more the chorus of voices went on with, "The man that drives the engine. Why, the smoke alone is worth a thousand pounds a puff!"

Alice thought to herself, "Then there's no use in speaking." The voices didn't join in *this* time, as she hadn't spoken, but, to her great surprise, they all *thought* in chorus (I hope you understand what *thinking in chorus* means —for I must confess that *I* don't), "Better say nothing at all. Language is worth a thousand pounds a word!"

"I shall dream about a thousand pounds to-night, I know I shall!" thought Alice.

All this time the Guard was looking at her, first through a telescope, then through a microscope, and then through an opera-glass. At last he said, "You're traveling the wrong way," and shut up the window and went away.

"So young a child," said the gentleman sitting opposite to her (he was dressed in white

"I don't know what you mean by *your* way,"
said the Queen:
"all the ways about here belong to *me*."

Page 28

The Guard was looking at her
through an opera-glass.
Page 40

LOOKING GLASS

paper), "ought to know which way she's going, even if she doesn't know her own name!"

A Goat, that was sitting next to the gentleman in white, shut his eyes and said in a loud voice, "She ought to know her way to the ticket-office, even if she doesn't know her alphabet!"

There was a Beetle sitting next the Goat (it was a very queer carriage-full of passengers altogether), and, as the rule seemed to be that they should all speak in turn, *he* went on with, "She'll have to go back from here as luggage!"

Alice couldn't see who was sitting beyond the Beetle, but a hoarse voice spoke next. "Change engines—" it said, and there it choked and was obliged to leave off.

"It sounds like a horse," Alice thought to herself. And an extremely small voice, close to her ear, said, <small>"You might make a joke on that—something about 'horse' and 'hoarse,' you know."</small>

Then a very gentle voice in the distance said, "She must be labeled, 'Lass, with care,' you know——"

[41]

And after that other voices went on ("What a number of people there are in the carriage!" thought Alice), saying, "She must go by post, as she's got a head on her—" "She must be sent as a message by the telegraph—" "She must draw the train herself the rest of the way—," and so on.

But the gentleman dressed in white paper leaned forwards and whispered in her ear, "Never mind what they all say, my dear, but take a return-ticket every time the train stops."

"Indeed I sha'n't!" Alice said rather impatiently. "I don't belong to this railway journey at all. I was in a wood just now—and I wish I could get back there!"

"You might make a joke on *that*," said the little voice close to her ear; "something about 'you *would* if you could,' you know."

"Don't tease so," said Alice, looking about in vain to see where the voice came from. "If you're so anxious to have a joke made, why don't you make one yourself?"

The little voice sighed deeply. It was *very* unhappy, evidently, and Alice would have said

[42]

something pitying to comfort it, "if it would only sigh like other people!" she thought. But this was such a wonderfully small sigh that she wouldn't have heard it at all if it hadn't come *quite* close to her ear. The consequence of this was that it tickled her ear very much, and quite took off her thoughts from the unhappiness of the poor little creature.

"I know you are a friend," the little voice went on; "a dear friend, and an old friend. And you won't hurt me, though I *am* an insect."

"What kind of insect?" Alice inquired, a little anxiously. What she really wanted to know was, whether it could sting or not, but she thought this wouldn't be quite a civil question to ask.

"What, then you don't——" the little voice began, when it was drowned by a shrill scream from the engine, and everybody jumped up in alarm, Alice among the rest.

The Horse, who had put his head out of the window, quietly drew it in and said, "It's only a brook we have to jump over." Everybody seemed satisfied with this, though Alice felt a

[43]

THROUGH THE

little nervous at the idea of trains jumping at all. "However, it'll take us into the Fourth Square, that's some comfort!" she said to herself. In another moment she felt the carriage rise straight up into the air, and in her fright she caught at the thing nearest to her hand, which happened to be the Goat's beard.

* * * * *

* * * *

* * * * *

But the beard seemed to melt away as she touched it, and she found herself sitting quietly under a tree—while the Gnat (for that was the insect she had been talking to) was balancing itself on a twig just over her head and fanning her with its wings.

It certainly was a *very* large Gnat; "about the size of a chicken," Alice thought. Still, she couldn't feel nervous with it, after they had been talking together so long.

"—then you don't like *all* insects?" the Gnat went on, as quietly as if nothing had happened.

"I like them when they can talk," Alice

[44]

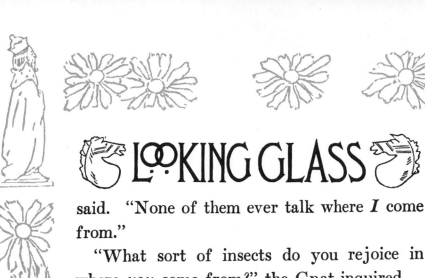

said. "None of them ever talk where *I* come from."

"What sort of insects do you rejoice in where *you* come from?" the Gnat inquired.

"I don't *rejoice* in insects at all," Alice explained, "because I'm rather afraid of them—at least the large kinds. But I can tell you the names of some of them."

"Of course they answer to their names?" the Gnat remarked carelessly.

"I never knew them to do it."

"What's the use of their having names," the Gnat said, "if they won't answer to them?"

"No use to *them,*" said Alice; "but it's useful to the people that name them, I suppose. If not, why do things have names at all?"

"I can't say," the Gnat replied. "Further on, in the wood down there, they've got no names—however, go on with your list of insects; you're wasting time."

"Well, there's the Horse-fly," Alice began, counting off the names on her fingers.

"All right," said the Gnat. "Half-way up

[45]

that bush you'll see a Rocking-horse-fly, if you look. It's made entirely of wood, and gets about by swinging itself from branch to branch."

"What does it live on?" Alice asked, with great curiosity.

"Sap and sawdust," said the Gnat. "Go on with the list."

Alice looked at the Rocking-horse-fly with great interest, and made up her mind that it must have been just repainted, it looked so bright and sticky; and then she went on.

"And there's the Dragon-fly."

"Look on the branch above your head," said the Gnat, "and there you'll find a Snap-dragon-fly. Its body is made of plum-pudding, its wings of holly-leaves, and its head is a raisin burning in brandy."

"And what does it live on?" Alice asked, as before.

"Frumenty and mince-pie," the Gnat replied; "and it makes its nest in a Christmas-box."

[46]

LOOKING GLASS

"And then there's the Butterfly," Alice went on, after she had taken a good look at the insect with its head on fire, and had thought to herself, "I wonder if that's the reason insects are so fond of flying into candles—because they want to turn into Snap-dragon-flies!"

"Crawling at your feet," said the Gnat (Alice drew her feet back in some alarm), "you may observe a Bread-and-butter-fly. Its wings are thin slices of bread-and-butter, its body is a crust, and its head is a lump of sugar."

"And what does *it* live on?"

"Weak tea with cream in it."

A new difficulty came into Alice's head. "Supposing it couldn't find any?" she suggested.

"Then it would die, of course."

"But that must happen very often," Alice remarked thoughtfully.

"It always happens," said the Gnat.

After this Alice was silent for a minute or two, pondering. The Gnat amused itself meanwhile by humming round and round her head:

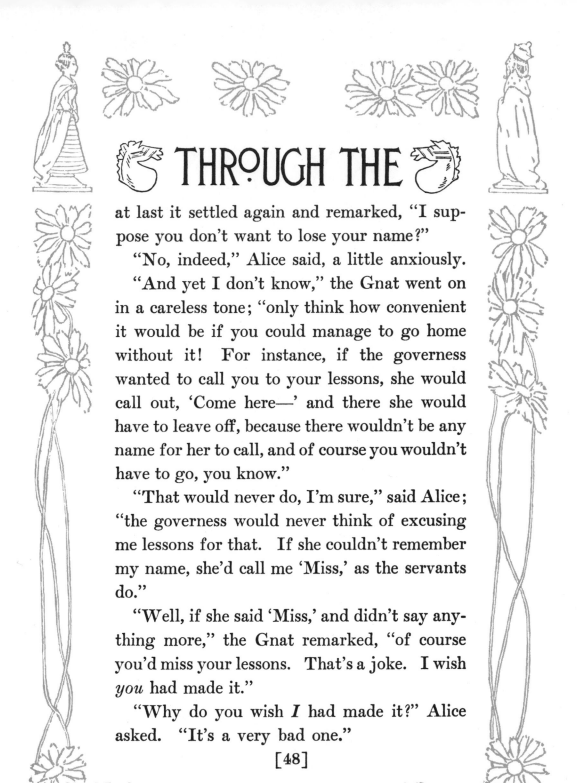

at last it settled again and remarked, "I suppose you don't want to lose your name?"

"No, indeed," Alice said, a little anxiously.

"And yet I don't know," the Gnat went on in a careless tone; "only think how convenient it would be if you could manage to go home without it! For instance, if the governess wanted to call you to your lessons, she would call out, 'Come here—' and there she would have to leave off, because there wouldn't be any name for her to call, and of course you wouldn't have to go, you know."

"That would never do, I'm sure," said Alice; "the governess would never think of excusing me lessons for that. If she couldn't remember my name, she'd call me 'Miss,' as the servants do."

"Well, if she said 'Miss,' and didn't say anything more," the Gnat remarked, "of course you'd miss your lessons. That's a joke. I wish *you* had made it."

"Why do you wish *I* had made it?" Alice asked. "It's a very bad one."

# LOOKING GLASS

But the Gnat only sighed deeply, while two large tears came rolling down its cheeks.

"You shouldn't make jokes," Alice said, "if it makes you so unhappy."

Then came another of those melancholy little sighs, and this time the poor Gnat really seemed to have sighed itself away, for when Alice looked up there was nothing whatever to be seen on the twig, and as she was getting quite chilly with sitting still so long, she got up and walked on.

She very soon came to an open field, with a wood on the other side of it; it looked much darker than the last wood, and Alice felt a *little* timid about going into it. However, on second thoughts, she made up her mind to go on: "for I certainly won't go *back,*" she thought to herself, and this was the only way to the Eighth Square.

"This must be the wood," she said thoughtfully to herself, "where things have no names. I wonder what'll become of *my* name when I go in? I shouldn't like to lose it at all—because

[49]

they'd have to give me another, and it would be almost certain to be an ugly one. But then the fun would be trying to find the creature that had got my old name! That's just like the advertisements, you know, when people lose dogs— *'answers to the name of "Dash"; had on a brass collar'*—just fancy calling everything you met 'Alice' till one of them answered! Only they wouldn't answer at all, if they were wise!"

She was rambling on in this way when she reached the wood; it looked very cool and shady. "Well, at any rate it's a great comfort," she said as she stepped under the trees, "after being so hot, to get into the—into the—into *what?*" she went on, rather surprised at not being able to think of the word. "I mean to get under the—under the—under *this,* you know!" putting her hand on the trunk of the tree. "What *does* it call itself, I wonder? I do believe it's got no name—why, to be sure it hasn't!"

She stood silent for a minute, thinking; then she suddenly began again. "Then it really *has* happened, after all! And now, who am I? I

# LOOKING GLASS

will remember, if I can! I'm determined to
do it!" But being determined didn't help her
much, and all she could say, after a great deal
of puzzling, was "L, I *know* it begins with L!"

Just then a Fawn came wandering by. It
looked at Alice with its large, gentle eyes, but
didn't seem at all frightened. "Here then! Here
then!" Alice said, as she held out her hand and
tried to stroke it; but it only started back a
little, and then stood looking at her again.

"What do you call yourself?" the Fawn said
at last. Such a soft, sweet voice it had!

"I wish I knew!" thought poor Alice. She
answered, rather sadly, "Nothing, just now."

"Think again," it said; "that won't do."

Alice thought, but nothing came of it.
"Please, would you tell me what *you* call yourself?" she said timidly. "I think that might
help a little."

"I'll tell you, if you'll come a little further
on," the Fawn said. "I can't remember *here*."

So they walked on together through the wood,
Alice with her arms clasped lovingly round the

 THROUGH THE

soft neck of the Fawn, till they came out into another open field, and here the Fawn gave a sudden bound into the air and shook itself free from Alice's arm. "I'm a Fawn!" it cried out in a voice of delight. "And, dear me! you're a human child!" A sudden look of alarm came into its beautiful brown eyes, and in another moment it had darted away at full speed.

Alice stood looking after it, almost ready to cry with vexation at having lost her dear little fellow-traveler so suddenly. "However, I know my name now," she said; "that's *some* comfort. Alice—Alice—I won't forget it again. And now, which of these finger-posts ought I to follow, I wonder?"

It was not a very difficult question to answer, as there was only one road through the wood, and the two finger-posts both pointed along it. "I'll settle it," Alice said to herself, "when the road divides and they point different ways."

But this did not seem likely to happen. She went on and on, a long way, but, wherever the road divided, there were sure to be two finger-

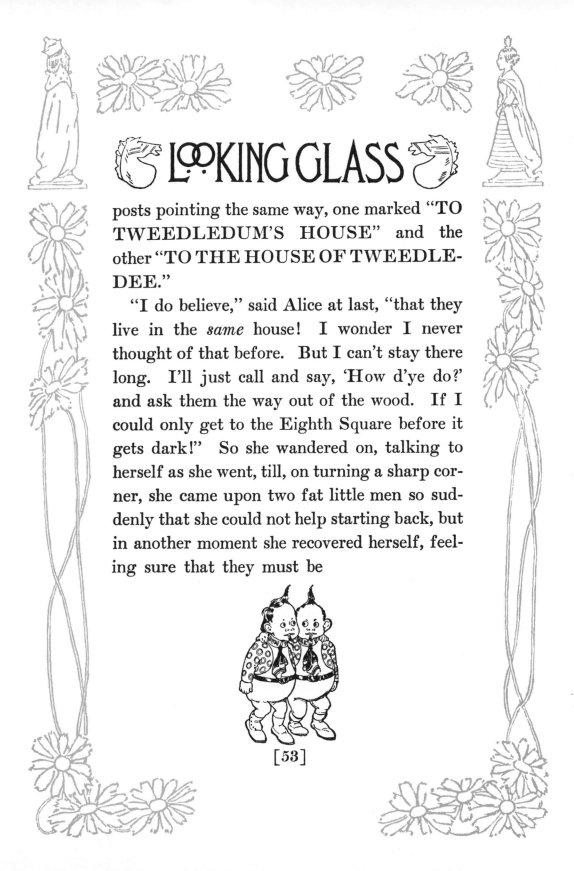

L☺KING GLASS

posts pointing the same way, one marked "TO TWEEDLEDUM'S HOUSE" and the other "TO THE HOUSE OF TWEEDLE-DEE."

"I do believe," said Alice at last, "that they live in the *same* house! I wonder I never thought of that before. But I can't stay there long. I'll just call and say, 'How d'ye do?' and ask them the way out of the wood. If I could only get to the Eighth Square before it gets dark!" So she wandered on, talking to herself as she went, till, on turning a sharp corner, she came upon two fat little men so suddenly that she could not help starting back, but in another moment she recovered herself, feeling sure that they must be

[53]

THROUGH THE

TWEEDLEDUM AND TWEEDLEDEE

THEY were standing under a tree, each with an arm round the other's neck, and Alice knew which was which in a moment, because one of them had "DUM" embroidered on his collar and the other "DEE." "I suppose they've each got 'TWEEDLE' round at the back of the collar," she said to herself.

They stood so still that she quite forgot they were alive, and she was just going round to see if the word "TWEEDLE" was written at the back of each collar when she was startled by a voice coming from the one marked "DUM."

"If you think we're wax-works," he said, "you ought to pay, you know. Wax-works weren't made to be looked at for nothing. No-how!"

"Contrariwise," added the one marked

# LOOKING GLASS

"DEE," "if you think we're alive, you ought to speak."

"I'm sure I'm very sorry," was all Alice could say; for the words of the old song kept ringing through her head like the ticking of a clock, and she could hardly help saying them out loud:

> *"Tweedledum and Tweedledee*
>   *Agreed to have a battle;*
> *For Tweedledum said Tweedledee*
>   *Had spoiled his nice new rattle.*
>
> *Just then flew down a monstrous crow,*
>   *As black as a tar-barrel;*
> *Which frightened both the heroes so,*
>   *They quite forgot their quarrel."*

"I know what you're thinking about," said Tweedledum; "but it isn't so, nohow."

"Contrariwise," continued Tweedledee, "if it was so, it might be; and if it were so, it would be; but as it isn't, it ain't. That's logic."

"I was thinking," Alice said very politely,

[55]

"which is the best way out of this wood; it's getting so dark. Would you tell me, please?"

But the fat little men only looked at each other and grinned.

They looked so exactly like a couple of great schoolboys that Alice couldn't help pointing her finger at Tweedledum and saying, "First Boy!"

"Nohow!" Tweedledum cried out briskly, and shut his mouth up again with a snap.

"Next Boy!" said Alice, passing on to Tweedledee, though she felt quite certain he would only shout out "Contrariwise!" and so he did.

"You've begun wrong!" cried Tweedledum. "The first thing in a visit is to say, 'How d'ye do?' and shake hands!" And here the two brothers gave each other a hug, and then they held out the two hands that were free, to shake hands with her.

Alice did not like shaking hands with either of them first, for fear of hurting the other one's

LOOKING GLASS

feelings; so, as the best way out of the diffi-culty, she took hold of both hands at once: the next moment they were dancing round in a ring. This seemed quite natural (she remem-bered afterwards), and she was not even sur-prised to hear music playing: it seemed to come from the tree under which they were dancing, and it was done (as well as she could make it out) by the branches rubbing one across the other, like fiddles and fiddle-sticks.

"But it certainly *was* funny" (Alice said afterwards, when she was telling her sister the history of all this) "to find myself singing, '*Here we go round the mulberry bush.*' I don't know when I began it, but somehow I felt as if I'd been singing it a long time!"

The other two dancers were fat, and very soon out of breath. "Four times round is enough for one dance," Tweedledum panted out, and they left off dancing as suddenly as they had begun; the music stopped at the same moment.

Then they let go of Alice's hands and stood

[57]

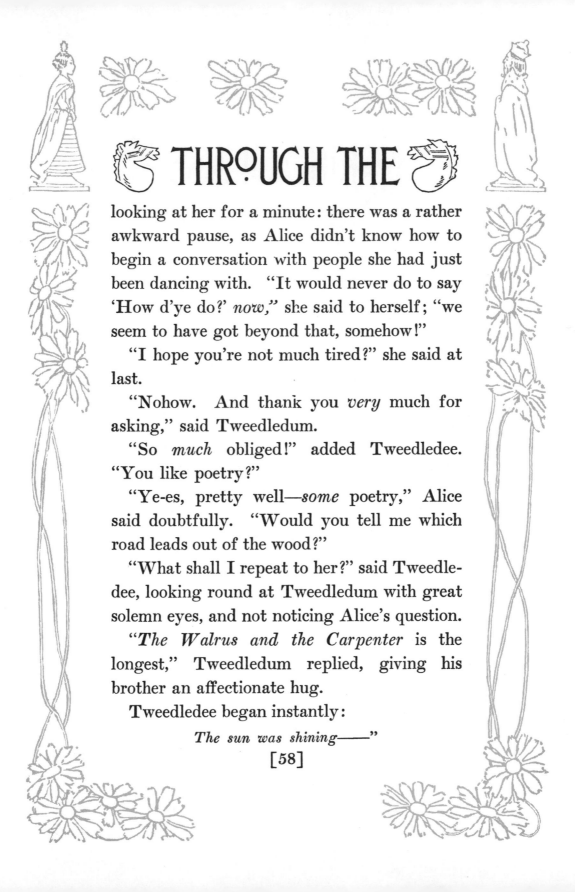

looking at her for a minute: there was a rather awkward pause, as Alice didn't know how to begin a conversation with people she had just been dancing with. "It would never do to say 'How d'ye do?' *now,*" she said to herself; "we seem to have got beyond that, somehow!"

"I hope you're not much tired?" she said at last.

"Nohow. And thank you *very* much for asking," said Tweedledum.

"So *much* obliged!" added Tweedledee. "You like poetry?"

"Ye-es, pretty well—*some* poetry," Alice said doubtfully. "Would you tell me which road leads out of the wood?"

"What shall I repeat to her?" said Tweedledee, looking round at Tweedledum with great solemn eyes, and not noticing Alice's question.

"*The Walrus and the Carpenter* is the longest," Tweedledum replied, giving his brother an affectionate hug.

Tweedledee began instantly:

The sun was shining——"

So they walked together through the wood,
Alice with her arms clasped lovingly
round the soft neck of the Fawn.

Page 51

They wept like anything to see
such quantities of sand.

Page 60

LKING GLASS

Here Alice ventured to interrupt him. "If it's *very* long," she said as politely as she could, "would you please tell me first which road——"

Tweedledee smiled gently, and began again:

"The sun was shining on the sea,
  Shining with all his might:
He did his very best to make
  The billows smooth and bright—
And this was odd, because it was
  The middle of the night.

"The moon was shining sulkily
  Because she thought the sun
Had got no business to be there
  After the day was done—
'It's very rude of him,' she said,
  'To come and spoil the fun!'

"The sea was wet as wet could be,
  The sands were dry as dry.
You could not see a cloud, because
  No cloud was in the sky:
No birds were flying overhead—
  There were no birds to fly.

THROUGH THE

"The Walrus and the Carpenter
　　Were walking close at hand:
They wept like anything to see
　　Such quantities of sand:
'If this were only cleared away,
　　They said, 'it would be grand!'

" 'If seven maids with seven mops
　　Swept it for half a year,
Do you suppose,' the Walrus said,
　　'That they could get it clear?'
'I doubt it,' said the Carpenter,
　　And shed a bitter tear.

" 'O Oysters, come and walk with us!'
　　The Walrus did beseech.
'A pleasant walk, a pleasant talk,
　　Along the briny beach:
We cannot do with more than four,
　　To give a hand to each.'

"The eldest Oyster looked at him,
　　But never a word he said:
The eldest Oyster winked his eye,
　　And shook his heavy head—
Meaning to say he did not choose
　　To leave the oyster-bed.

[60]

# LOOKING GLASS

"But four young Oysters hurried up,
    All eager for the treat:
Their coats were brushed, their faces washed,
    Their shoes were clean and neat—
And this was odd, because, you know,
    They hadn't any feet.

"Four other Oysters followed them,
    And yet another four;
And thick and fast they came at last,
    And more, and more, and more—
All hopping through the frothy waves,
    And scrambling to the shore.

"The Walrus and the Carpenter
    Walked on a mile or so,
And then they rested on a rock
    Conveniently low:
And all the little Oysters stood
    And waited in a row.

" 'The time has come,' the Walrus said,
    'To talk of many things:
Of shoes—and ships—and sealing-wax—
    Of cabbages—and kings—
And why the sea is boiling hot—
    And whether pigs have wings.'

[61]

# THROUGH THE

" 'But wait a bit,' the Oysters cried,
    'Before we have our chat;
For some of us are out of breath,
    And all of us are fat!'
'No hurry!' said the Carpenter.
    They thanked him much for that.

" 'A loaf of bread,' the Walrus said,
    'Is what we chiefly need:
Pepper and vinegar besides
    Are very good indeed—
Now, if you're ready, Oysters dear,
    We can begin to feed.'

" 'But not on us!' the Oysters cried,
    Turning a little blue.
'After such kindness, that would be
    A dismal thing to do!'
'The night is fine,' the Walrus said.
    'Do you admire the view?

" 'It was so kind of you to come!
    And you are very nice!'
The Carpenter said nothing but
    'Cut us another slice.
I wish you were not quite so deaf—
    I've had to ask you twice!'

[62]

LOOKING GLASS

"'It seems a shame,' the Walrus said,
    'To play them such a trick.
After we've brought them out so far,
    And made them trot so quick!'
The Carpenter said nothing but
    'The butter's spread too thick!'

"'I weep for you,' the Walrus said:
    'I deeply sympathize.'
With sobs and tears he sorted out
    Those of the largest size
Holding his pocket-handkerchief
    Before his streaming eyes.

"'O Oysters,' said the Carpenter,
    'You've had a pleasant run!
Shall we be trotting home again?'
    But answer came there none—
And this was scarcely odd, because
    They'd eaten every one."

"I like the Walrus best," said Alice, "because he was a *little* sorry for the poor oysters."

"He ate more than the Carpenter, though," said Tweedledee. "You see he held his handkerchief in front, so that the Carpenter couldn't count how many he took; contrariwise."

"That was mean!" Alice said indignantly. "Then I like the Carpenter best—if he didn't eat so many as the Walrus."

"But he ate as many as he could get," said Tweedledum.

This was a puzzler. After a pause Alice began, "Well, they were *both* very unpleasant characters—" Here she checked herself in some alarm at hearing something that sounded to her like the puffing of a large steam-engine in the wood near them, though she feared it was more likely to be a wild beast. "Are there any lions or tigers about here?" she asked timidly.

"It's only the Red King snoring," said Tweedledee.

"Come and look at him!" the brothers cried, and they each took one of Alice's hands and led her up to where the King was sleeping.

"Isn't he a *lovely* sight?" said Tweedledum.

Alice couldn't say honestly that he was. He had a tall red night-cap on, with a tassel, and he was lying crumpled up into a sort of

 # LOOKING GLASS

untidy heap, and snoring loud—"fit to snore his head off!" as Tweedledum remarked.

"I'm afraid he'll catch cold with lying on the damp grass," said Alice, who was a very thoughtful little girl.

"He's dreaming now," said Tweedledee; "and what do you think he's dreaming about?"

Alice said, "Nobody can guess that."

"Why, about *you!*" Tweedledee exclaimed, clapping his hands triumphantly. "And if he left off dreaming about you, where do you suppose you'd be?"

"Where I am now, of course," said Alice.

"Not you!" Tweedledee retorted contemptuously. "You'd be nowhere. Why, you're only a sort of thing in his dream!"

"If that there King was to wake," added Tweedledum, "you'd go out—bang!—just like a candle!"

"I shouldn't!" Alice exclaimed indignantly. "Besides, if *I'm* only a sort of thing in his dream, what are *you,* I should like to know?"

"Ditto," said Tweedledum.

[65]

"Ditto, ditto!" cried Tweedledee.

He shouted this so loud that Alice couldn't help saying, "Hush! You'll be waking him, I'm afraid, if you make so much noise."

"Well, it's no use *your* talking about waking him," said Tweedledum, "when you're only one of the things in his dream. You know very well you're not real."

"I *am* real!" said Alice, and began to cry.

"You won't make yourself a bit realler by crying," Tweedledee remarked; "there's nothing to cry about."

"If I wasn't real," Alice said—half laughing through her tears, it all seemed so ridiculous— "I shouldn't be able to cry."

"I hope you don't suppose those are *real* tears?" Tweedledum interrupted in a tone of great contempt.

"I know they're talking nonsense," Alice thought to herself, "and it's foolish to cry about it." So she brushed away her tears, and went on as cheerfully as she could, "At any rate, I'd better be getting out of the wood, for

really it's coming on very dark. Do you think it's going to rain?"

Tweedledum spread a large umbrella over himself and his brother, and looked up into it. "No, I don't think it is," he said; "at least—not under *here*. Nohow."

"But it may rain *outside?*"

"It may—if it chooses," said Tweedledee; "we've no objection. Contrariwise."

"Selfish things!" thought Alice, and she was just going to say "Good-night" and leave them when Tweedledum sprang out from under the umbrella and seized her by the wrist.

"Do you see *that?*" he said, in a voice choking with passion, and his eyes grew large and yellow all in a moment, as he pointed with a trembling finger at a small white thing lying under the tree.

"It's only a rattle," Alice said, after a careful examination of the little white thing. "Not a rattle-*snake,* you know," she added hastily, thinking that he was frightened; "only an old rattle—quite old and broken."

[67]

"I knew it was!" cried Tweedledum, beginning to stamp about wildly and tear his hair. "It's spoilt, of course!" Here he looked at Tweedledee, who immediately sat down on the ground and tried to hide himself under the umbrella.

Alice laid her hand upon his arm, and said, in a soothing tone, "You needn't be so angry about an old rattle."

"But it *isn't* old!" Tweedledum cried, in a greater fury than ever. "It's *new,* I tell you—I bought it yesterday—my nice NEW RATTLE!" and his voice rose to a perfect scream.

All this time Tweedledee was trying his best to fold up the umbrella, with himself in it; which was such an extraordinary thing to do

[68]

She floated gently down without even touching
the stairs with her feet.

Page 19

And all the little Oysters stood
And waited in a row.

Page 61

# LOOKING GLASS

that it quite took off Alice's attention from the angry brother. But he couldn't quite succeed, and it ended in his rolling over, bundled up in the umbrella, with only his head out; and there he lay, opening and shutting his mouth and his large eyes—"looking more like a fish than anything else," Alice thought.

"Of course you agree to have a battle?" Tweedledum said in a calmer tone.

"I suppose so," the other sulkily replied, as he crawled out of the umbrella; "only *she* must help us to dress up, you know."

So the two brothers went off hand-in-hand into the wood, and returned in a minute with their arms full of things—such as bolsters, blankets, hearth-rugs, tablecloths, dish-covers, and coal-scuttles. "I hope you're a good hand at pinning and tying strings?" Tweedledum remarked. "Every one of these things has got to go on, somehow or other."

Alice said afterwards she had never seen such a fuss made about anything in all her life —the way those two bustled about—and the

[69]

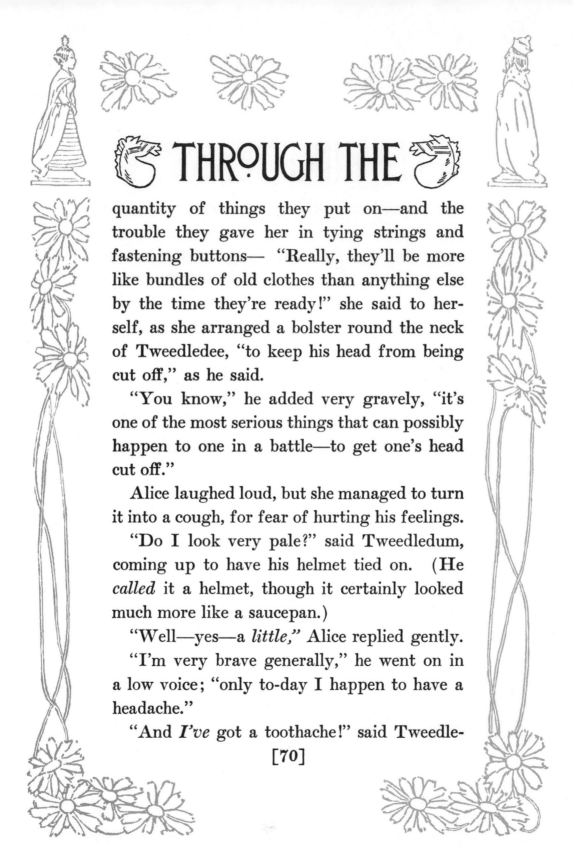

quantity of things they put on—and the trouble they gave her in tying strings and fastening buttons— "Really, they'll be more like bundles of old clothes than anything else by the time they're ready!" she said to herself, as she arranged a bolster round the neck of Tweedledee, "to keep his head from being cut off," as he said.

"You know," he added very gravely, "it's one of the most serious things that can possibly happen to one in a battle—to get one's head cut off."

Alice laughed loud, but she managed to turn it into a cough, for fear of hurting his feelings.

"Do I look very pale?" said Tweedledum, coming up to have his helmet tied on. (He *called* it a helmet, though it certainly looked much more like a saucepan.)

"Well—yes—a *little*," Alice replied gently.

"I'm very brave generally," he went on in a low voice; "only to-day I happen to have a headache."

"And *I've* got a toothache!" said Tweedle-

dee, who had overheard the remark. "I'm far worse than you!"

"Then you'd better not fight to-day," said Alice, thinking it a good opportunity to make peace.

"We *must* have a bit of a fight, but I don't care about going on long," said Tweedledum. "What's the time now?"

Tweedledee looked at his watch and said, "Half-past four."

"Let's fight till six, and then have dinner," said Tweedledum.

"Very well," the other said, rather sadly; "and *she* can watch us—only you'd better not come *very* close," he added; "I generally hit everything I can see—when I get really excited."

"And *I* hit everything within reach," cried Tweedledum, "whether I can see it or not!"

Alice laughed. "You must hit the *trees* pretty often, I should think," she said.

Tweedledum looked round him with a satisfied smile. "I don't suppose," he said, "there'll

be a tree left standing for ever so far round by the time we've finished!"

"And all about a rattle!" said Alice, still hoping to make them a *little* ashamed of fighting for such a trifle.

"I shouldn't have minded it so much," said Tweedledum, "if it hadn't been a new one."

"I wish the monstrous crow would come!" thought Alice.

"There's only one sword, you know," Tweedledum said to his brother; "but *you* can have the umbrella—it's quite as sharp. Only we must begin quick. It's getting as dark as it can."

"And darker," said Tweedledee.

It was getting dark so suddenly that Alice thought there must be a thunderstorm coming on. "What a thick black cloud that is!" she said. "And how fast it comes! Why, I do believe it's got wings!"

"It's the crow!" Tweedledum cried out in a shrill voice of alarm; and the two brothers

# LOOKING GLASS

took to their heels and were out of sight in **a** moment.

Alice ran a little way into the wood, and stopped under a large tree. "It can never get at me *here*," she thought; "it's far too large to squeeze itself in among the trees. But I wish it wouldn't flap its wings so—it makes quite a hurricane in the wood—here's somebody's shawl being blown away!"

THROUGH THE

WOOL AND WATER

SHE caught the shawl as she spoke, and looked about for the owner. In another moment the White Queen came running wildly through the wood, with both arms stretched out wide, as if she were flying, and Alice very civilly went to meet her with the shawl.

"I'm very glad I happened to be in the way," Alice said, as she helped her to put on her shawl again.

The White Queen only looked at her in a helpless, frightened sort of way, and kept repeating something in a whisper to herself that sounded like "Bread-and-butter, bread-and-butter," and Alice felt that if there was to be any conversation at all, she must manage it herself. So she began rather timidly: "Am I addressing the White Queen?"

[74]

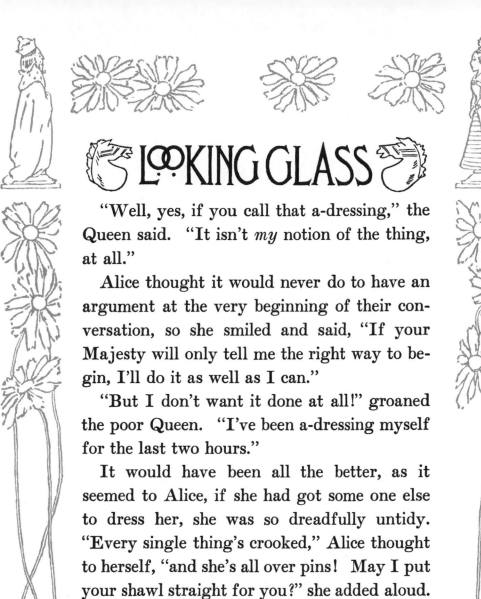

LOOKING GLASS

"Well, yes, if you call that a-dressing," the Queen said. "It isn't *my* notion of the thing, at all."

Alice thought it would never do to have an argument at the very beginning of their conversation, so she smiled and said, "If your Majesty will only tell me the right way to begin, I'll do it as well as I can."

"But I don't want it done at all!" groaned the poor Queen. "I've been a-dressing myself for the last two hours."

It would have been all the better, as it seemed to Alice, if she had got some one else to dress her, she was so dreadfully untidy. "Every single thing's crooked," Alice thought to herself, "and she's all over pins! May I put your shawl straight for you?" she added aloud.

"I don't know what's the matter with it!" the Queen said, in a melancholy voice. "It's out of temper, I think. I've pinned it here, and I've pinned it there, but there's no pleasing it!"

"It *can't* go straight, you know, if you pin

 THROUGH THE

it all on one side," Alice said, as she gently put it right for her; "and, dear me, what a state your hair is in!"

"The brush has got entangled in it!" the Queen said with a sigh. "And I lost the comb yesterday."

Alice carefully released the brush, and did her best to get the hair into order. "Come, you look rather better now!" she said, after altering most of the pins. "But really, you should have a lady's-maid!"

"I'm sure I'll take *you* with pleasure!" the Queen said. "Twopence a week, and jam every other day."

Alice couldn't help laughing, as she said, "I don't want you to hire *me*—and I don't care for jam."

"It's very good jam," said the Queen.

"Well, I don't want any *to-day,* at any rate."

"You couldn't have it if you *did* want it," the Queen said. "The rule is, jam to-morrow and jam yesterday—but never jam *to-day.*"

[76]

 LOOKING GLASS

"It *must* come sometimes to 'jam to-day,'" Alice objected.

"No, it can't," said the Queen. "It's jam every *other* day; to-day isn't any *other* day, you know."

"I don't understand you," said Alice. "It's dreadfully confusing!"

"That's the effect of living backwards," the Queen said kindly: "it always makes one a little giddy at first——"

"Living backwards!" Alice repeated in great astonishment. "I never heard of such a thing!"

"——but there's one great advantage in it, that one's memory works both ways."

"I'm sure *mine* only works one way," Alice remarked. "I can't remember things before they happen."

"It's a poor sort of memory that only works backwards," the Queen remarked.

"What sort of things do *you* remember best?" Alice ventured to ask.

"Oh, things that happened the week after next," the Queen replied in a careless tone.

[77]

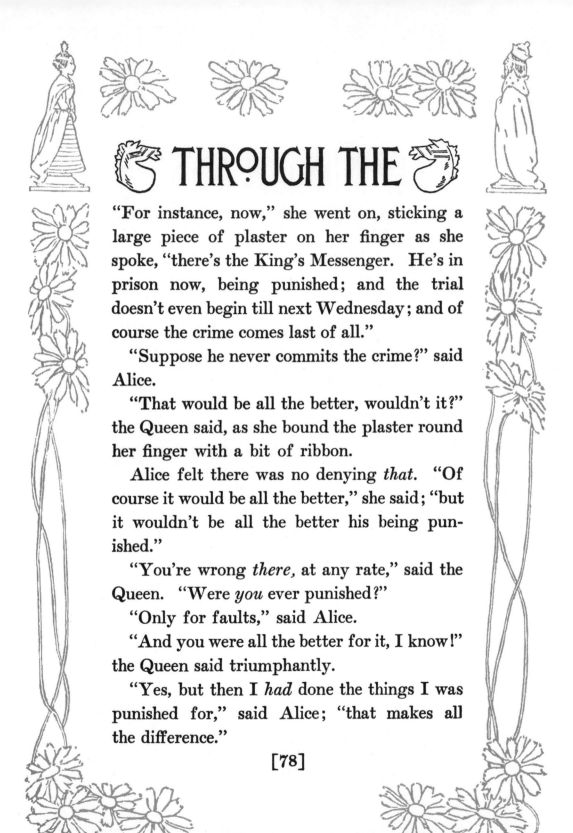

"For instance, now," she went on, sticking a large piece of plaster on her finger as she spoke, "there's the King's Messenger. He's in prison now, being punished; and the trial doesn't even begin till next Wednesday; and of course the crime comes last of all."

"Suppose he never commits the crime?" said Alice.

"That would be all the better, wouldn't it?" the Queen said, as she bound the plaster round her finger with a bit of ribbon.

Alice felt there was no denying *that*. "Of course it would be all the better," she said; "but it wouldn't be all the better his being punished."

"You're wrong *there,* at any rate," said the Queen. "Were *you* ever punished?"

"Only for faults," said Alice.

"And you were all the better for it, I know!" the Queen said triumphantly.

"Yes, but then I *had* done the things I was punished for," said Alice; "that makes all the difference."

[78]

# LOOKING GLASS

"But if you *hadn't* done them," the Queen said, "that would have been better still; better, and better, and better!" Her voice went higher with each "better," till it got quite to a squeak at last.

Alice was just beginning to say, "There's a mistake somewhere—" when the Queen began screaming so loud that she had to leave the sentence unfinished. "Oh, oh, oh!" shouted the Queen, shaking her hand about as if she wanted to shake it off. "My finger's bleeding! Oh, oh, oh, oh!"

Her screams were so exactly like the whistle of a steam-engine, that Alice had to hold both her hands over her ears.

"What *is* the matter?" she said, as soon as there was a chance of making herself heard. "Have you pricked your finger?"

"I haven't pricked it *yet*," the Queen said, "but I soon shall—oh, oh, oh!"

"When do you expect to do it?"

[79]

Alice asked, feeling very much inclined to laugh.

"When I fasten my shawl again," the poor Queen groaned out; "the brooch will come undone directly. Oh, oh!" As she said the words the brooch flew open, and the Queen clutched wildly at it and tried to clasp it again.

"Take care!" cried Alice. "You're holding it all crooked!" And she caught at the brooch; but it was too late: the pin had slipped and the Queen had pricked her finger.

"That accounts for the bleeding, you see," she said to Alice with a smile. "Now you understand the way things happen here."

"But why don't you scream *now?*" Alice asked, holding her hands ready to put over her ears again.

"Why, I've done all the screaming already," said the Queen. "What would be the good of having it all over again?"

By this time it was getting light. "The crow must have flown away, I think," said Alice;

[80]

 LOOKING GLASS

"I'm so glad it's gone. I thought it was the night coming on."

"I wish *I* could manage to be glad!" the Queen said. "Only I never can remember the rule. You must be very happy, living in this wood, and being glad whenever you like!"

"Only it is so *very* lonely here!" Alice said in a melancholy voice; and at the thought of her loneliness two large tears came rolling down her cheeks.

"Oh, don't go on like that!" cried the poor Queen, ringing her hands in despair. "Consider what a great girl you are. Consider what a long way you've come to-day. Consider what o'clock it is. Consider anything, only don't cry!"

Alice could not help laughing at this, even in the midst of her tears. "Can *you* keep from crying by considering things?" she asked.

"That's the way it's done," the Queen said with great decision; "nobody can do two things at once, you know. Let's consider your age to begin with—how old are you?"

"I'm seven and a half, exactly."

"You needn't say 'exactually,'" the Queen remarked. "I can believe it without that. Now I'll give *you* something to believe. I'm just one hundred and one, five months and a day."

"I can't believe *that!*" said Alice.

"Can't you?" the Queen said in a pitying tone. "Try again; draw a long breath and shut your eyes."

Alice laughed. "There's no use trying," she said; one *can't* believe impossible things."

"I daresay you haven't had much practice," said the Queen. "When I was your age I always did it for half-an-hour a day. Why, sometimes I've believed as many as six impossible things before breakfast. There goes the shawl again!"

The brooch had come undone as she spoke, and a sudden gust of wind blew the Queen's shawl across a little brook. The Queen spread out her arms again, and went flying after it, and this time she succeeded in catching it for herself. "I've got it!" she cried in a triumphant

[82]

tone. "Now you shall see me pin it on **again**, all by myself!"

"Then I hope your finger is better now?" Alice said very politely, as she crossed the little brook after the Queen.

*   *   *   *   *   *
*   *   *   *   *
*   *   *   *   *   *

"Oh, much better!" cried the Queen, her voice rising into a squeak as she went on. "Much be-etter! Be-etter! Be-e-e-etter! Be-e-ehh!" The last word ended in a long bleat, so like a sheep that Alice quite started.

She looked at the Queen, who seemed to have suddenly wrapped herself up in wool. Alice rubbed her eyes and looked again. She couldn't make out what had happened at all. Was she in a shop? And was that really—was it really a *sheep* that was sitting on the other side of the counter? Rub as she would, she could make nothing more of it: she was in a little dark shop, leaning with her elbows on the counter, and opposite to her was an old

[83]

THROUGH THE

Sheep, sitting in an arm-chair, knitting, and every now and then leaving off to look at her through a great pair of spectacles.

"What is it you want to buy?" the Sheep said at last, looking up for a moment from her knitting.

"I don't *quite* know yet," Alice said very gently. "I should like to look all round me first, if I might."

"You may look in front of you and on both sides, if you like," said the Sheep; "but you can't look *all* round you—unless you've got eyes at the back of your head."

But these, as it happened, Alice had *not* got; so she contented herself with turning round, looking at the shelves as she came to them.

The shop seemed to be full of all manner of curious things—but the oddest part of it all was that, whenever she looked hard at any shelf, to make out exactly what it had on it, that particular shelf was always quite empty, though the others round it were crowded as full as they could hold.

[84]

# LOOKING GLASS

"Things flow about so here!" she said at last in a plaintive tone, after she had spent a minute or so in vainly pursuing a large bright thing, that looked sometimes like a doll and sometimes like a work-box, and was always in the shelf next above the one she was looking at. "And this one is the most provoking of all— but I'll tell you what—" she added, as a sudden thought struck her. "I'll follow it up to the very top shelf of all. It'll puzzle it to go through the ceiling, I expect!"

But even this plan failed: the "thing" went through the ceiling as quietly as possible, as if it were quite used to it.

"Are you a child or a teetotum?" the Sheep said, as she took up another pair of needles. "You'll make me giddy soon, if you go on turning round like that." She was now working with fourteen pairs at once, and Alice couldn't help looking at her in great astonishment.

"How *can* she knit with so many?" the puzzled child thought to herself. "She gets

[85]

more and more like a porcupine every minute!"

"Can you row?" the Sheep asked, handing her a pair of knitting-needles as she spoke.

"Yes, a little—but not on land—and not with needles—" Alice was beginning to say, when suddenly the needles turned into oars in her hands, and she found they were in a little boat, gliding along between banks; so there was nothing for it but to do her best.

"Feather!" cried the Sheep, as she took up another pair of needles.

This didn't sound like a remark that needed any answer; so Alice said nothing, but pulled away. There was something very queer about the water, she thought, as every now and then the oars got fast in it and would hardly come out again.

"Feather! Feather!" the Sheep cried again, taking more needles. "You'll be catching a crab directly."

"A dear little crab!" thought Alice. "I should like that."

"Didn't you hear me say 'Feather'?" the Sheep cried angrily, taking up quite a bunch of needles.

"Indeed I did," said Alice; "you've said it very often—and very loud. Please, where *are* the crabs?"

"In the water, of course!" said the Sheep, sticking some of the needles into her hair, as her hands were full. "Feather, I say!"

"*Why* do you say 'Feather' so often?" Alice asked at last, rather vexed. "I'm not a bird!"

"You are," said the Sheep; "you're a little goose."

This offended Alice a little, so there was no more conversation for a minute or two, while the boat glided gently on, sometimes among beds of weeds (which made the oars stick fast in the water, worse than ever), and sometimes under trees, but always with the same tall river-banks frowning over their heads.

"Oh, please! There are some scented rushes!" Alice cried in a sudden transport

[87]

# THROUGH THE

of delight. "There really are—and *such*
beauties!"

"You needn't say 'please' to *me* about 'em,"
the Sheep said, without looking up from her
knitting; "I didn't put 'em there, and I'm not
going to take 'em away."

"No, but I meant—please, may we wait and
pick some?" Alice pleaded. "If you don't mind
stopping the boat for a minute."

"How am *I* to stop it?" said the Sheep. "If
you leave off rowing, it'll stop of itself."

So the boat was left to drift down the stream
as it would, till it glided gently in among the
waving rushes. And then the little sleeves were
carefully rolled up, and the little arms were
plunged in elbow-deep, to get hold of the rushes
a good long way down before breaking them
off—and for a while Alice forgot all about the
Sheep and the knitting, as she bent over the
side of the boat, with just the ends of her
tangled hair dipping into the water—while
with bright, eager eyes she caught at one bunch
after another of the darling scented rushes.

# L**OO**KING GLASS

"I only hope the boat won't topple over!" she said to herself. "Oh, *what* a lovely one! Only I couldn't quite reach it." And it certainly *did* seem a little provoking ("almost as if it happened on purpose," she thought) that, though she managed to pick plenty of beautiful rushes as the boat glided by, there was always a more lovely one that she couldn't reach.

"The prettiest are always further!" she said at last, with a sigh at the obstinacy of the rushes in growing so far off, as, with flushed cheeks and dripping hair and hands, she scrambled back into her place and began to arrange her new-found treasures.

What mattered it to her just then that the rushes had begun to fade and to lose all their scent and beauty from the very moment that she picked them? Even real scented rushes, you know, last only a very little while—and these, being dream-rushes, melted away almost like snow, as they lay in heaps at her feet— but Alice hardly noticed this, there were so many other curious things to think about.

[89]

 # THROUGH THE

They hadn't gone much farther before the blade of one of the oars got fast in the water and *wouldn't* come out again (so Alice explained it afterwards), and the consequence was that the handle of it caught her under the chin, and, in spite of a series of little shrieks of "Oh, oh, oh!" from poor Alice, it swept her straight off the seat and down among the heap of rushes.

However, she wasn't a bit hurt, and was soon up again. The Sheep went on with her knitting all the while, just as if nothing had happened. "That was a nice crab you caught!" she remarked as Alice got back into her place, very much relieved to find herself still in the boat.

"Was it? I didn't see it," said Alice, peeping cautiously over the side of the boat into the dark water. "I wish it hadn't let go—I should so like a little crab to take home with me!" But the Sheep only laughed scornfully and went on with her knitting.

"Are there many crabs here?" said Alice.

"Crabs and all sorts of things," said the

Opposite to her was an old Sheep.

Page 85

The oars, and the boat, and the river
had vanished all in a moment.

Page 91

 # LOOKING GLASS

Sheep; "plenty of choice, only make up your mind.   Now, what *do* you want to buy?"

"To buy!" Alice echoed in a tone that was half astonished and half frightened, for the oars, and the boat, and the river had vanished all in a moment, and she was back again in the little dark shop.

"I should like to buy an egg, please," she said timidly.   "How do you sell them?"

"Fivepence farthing for one—twopence for two," the Sheep replied.

"Then two are cheaper than one?" Alice said in a surprised tone, taking out her purse.

"Only you *must* eat them both if you buy two," said the Sheep.

"Then I'll have *one,* please," said Alice, as she put the money down on the counter.   For she thought to herself, "They mightn't be at all nice, you know."

The Sheep took the money and put it away in a box; then she said, "I never put things into people's hands—that would never do—you must get it for yourself."   And so saying, she

[91]

went off to the other end of the shop and set the egg upright on a shelf.

"I wonder *why* it wouldn't do?" thought Alice, as she groped her way among the tables and chairs, for the shop was very dark towards the end. "The egg seems to get further away the more I walk towards it. Let me see, is this a chair? Why, it's got branches, I declare! How very odd to find trees growing here! And actually here's a little brook! Well, this is the very queerest shop I ever saw!"

* * * * * *

* * * * *

* * * * * *

So she went on, wondering more and more at every step, as everything turned into a tree the moment she came up to it, and she quite expected the egg to do the same.

LKING GLASS

HUMPTY DUMPTY

HOWEVER, the egg only got larger and larger and more and more human; when she had come within a few yards of it she saw that it had eyes and a nose and mouth; and when she had come close to it, she saw clearly that it was HUMPTY DUMPTY himself. "It can't be anybody else!" she said to herself. "I'm as certain of it as if his name were written all over his face!"

It might have been written a hundred times easily on that enormous face. Humpty Dumpty was sitting, with his legs crossed like a Turk, on the top of a high wall—such a narrow one that Alice quite wondered how he could keep his balance—and as his eyes were steadily fixed in the opposite direction, and he didn't take the least notice of her, she thought he must be a stuffed figure, after all.

[93]

"And how exactly like an egg he is!" she said aloud, standing with her hands ready to catch him, for she was every moment expecting him to fall.

"It's *very* provoking," Humpty Dumpty said after a long silence, looking away from Alice as he spoke, "to be called an egg—*very!*"

"I said you *looked* like an egg, Sir," Alice gently explained. "And some eggs are very pretty, you know," she added, hoping to turn her remark into a sort of compliment.

"Some people," said Humpty Dumpty, looking away from her as usual, "have no more sense than a baby!"

Alice didn't know what to say to this: it wasn't at all like conversation, she thought, as he never said anything to *her;* in fact, his last remark was evidently addressed to a tree—so she stood and softly repeated to herself:

"Humpty Dumpty sat on a wall:
Humpty Dumpty had a great fall.
All the King's horses and all the King's men
Couldn't put Humpty Dumpty in his place again."

[94]

# LOOKING GLASS

"That last line is much too long for the poetry," she added almost out loud, forgetting that Humpty Dumpty would hear her.

"Don't stand chattering to yourself like that," Humpty Dumpty said, looking at her for the first time, "but tell me your name and your business."

"My *name* is Alice, but——"

"It's a stupid name enough!" Humpty Dumpty interrupted impatiently. "What does it mean?"

"*Must* a name mean something?" Alice asked doubtfully.

"Of course it must," Humpty Dumpty said with a short laugh; *my* name means the shape I am—and a good handsome shape it is, too. With a name like yours, you might be any shape, almost."

"Why do you sit out here all alone?" said Alice, not wishing to begin an argument.

"Why, because there's nobody with me!" cried Humpty Dumpty. "Did you think I didn't know the answer to *that?* Ask another."

[95]

"Don't you think you'd be safer down on the ground?" Alice went on, not with any idea of making another riddle, but simply in her good-natured anxiety for the queer creature. "That wall is so *very* narrow!"

"What tremendously easy riddles you ask!" Humpty Dumpty growled out. "Of course I don't think so! Why, if ever I *did* fall off—which there's no chance of—but *if* I did—" Here he pursed up his lips and looked so solemn and grand that Alice could hardly help laughing. *"If* I *did* fall," he went on, *"the King has promised me*—ah, you may turn pale, if you like! You didn't think I was going to say that, did you? *The King has promised me—with his very own mouth—to—to——"*

"To send all his horses and all his men," Alice interrupted, rather unwisely.

"Now I declare that's too bad!" Humpty Dumpty cried, breaking into a sudden passion. "You've been listening at doors—and behind trees—and down chimneys—or you couldn't have known it!"

"I haven't, indeed!" Alice said very gently. "It's in a book."

"Ah, well! They may write such things in a *book*," Humpty Dumpty said in a calmer tone. "That's what you call a History of England, that is. Now, take a good look at me! I'm one that has spoken to a King, *I* am; mayhap you'll never see such another; and to show you I'm not proud, you may shake hands with me!" And he grinned almost from ear to ear as he leant forwards (and as nearly as possible fell off the wall in doing so) and offered Alice his hand. She watched him a little anxiously as she took it. "If he smiled much more the ends of his mouth might meet behind," she thought; "and then I don't know *what* would happen to his head! I'm afraid it would come off!"

"Yes, all his horses and all his men," Humpty Dumpty went on. "They'd

[97]

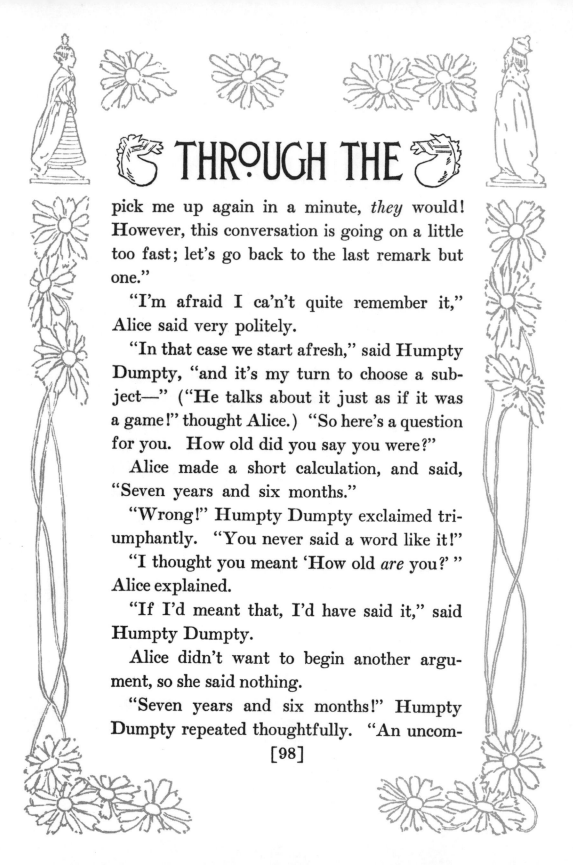

pick me up again in a minute, *they* would! However, this conversation is going on a little too fast; let's go back to the last remark but one."

"I'm afraid I ca'n't quite remember it," Alice said very politely.

"In that case we start afresh," said Humpty Dumpty, "and it's my turn to choose a subject—" ("He talks about it just as if it was a game!" thought Alice.) "So here's a question for you. How old did you say you were?"

Alice made a short calculation, and said, "Seven years and six months."

"Wrong!" Humpty Dumpty exclaimed triumphantly. "You never said a word like it!"

"I thought you meant 'How old *are* you?'" Alice explained.

"If I'd meant that, I'd have said it," said Humpty Dumpty.

Alice didn't want to begin another argument, so she said nothing.

"Seven years and six months!" Humpty Dumpty repeated thoughtfully. "An uncom-

[98]

He called it a helmet,
though it looked like a saucepan.

Page 70

The little arms were plunged in elbow deep.

Page 88

fortable sort of age. Now if you'd asked *my* advice, I'd have said, 'Leave off at seven,' but it's too late now."

"I never ask advice about growing," Alice said indignantly.

"Too proud?" the other inquired.

Alice felt even more indignant at this suggestion. "I mean," she said, "that one can't help growing older."

"*One* can't, perhaps," said Humpty Dumpty; "but *two* can. With proper assistance, you might have left off at seven."

"What a beautiful belt you've got on!" Alice suddenly remarked. (They had had quite enough of the subject of age, she thought, and if they really were to take turns in choosing subjects, it was *her* turn now.) "At least," she corrected herself on second thoughts, "a beautiful cravat, I should have said—no, a belt, I mean—I beg your pardon!" she added in dismay, for Humpty Dumpty looked thoroughly offended, and she began to wish she hadn't chosen that subject. "If only I knew,"

[99]

she thought to herself, "which was neck and which was waist!"

Evidently Humpty Dumpty was very angry, though he said nothing for a minute or two. When he *did* speak again, it was in a deep growl.

"It is a—*most*—*provoking*—thing," he said at last, "when a person doesn't know a cravat from a belt!"

"I know it's very ignorant of me," Alice said in so humble a tone that Humpty Dumpty relented.

"It's a cravat, child, and a beautiful one, as you say. It's a present from the White King and Queen. There now!"

"Is it really?" said Alice, quite pleased to find that she *had* chosen a good subject after all.

"They gave it me," Humpty Dumpty continued thoughtfully, as he crossed one knee over the other and clasped his hands round it—"they gave it me for an un-birthday present."

"I beg your pardon?" Alice said with a puzzled air.

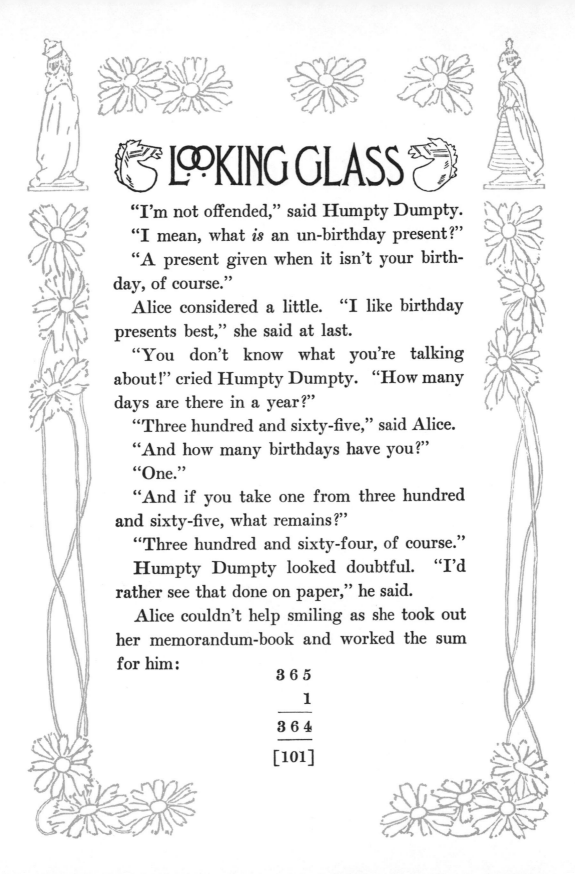

LOOKING GLASS

"I'm not offended," said Humpty Dumpty.

"I mean, what *is* an un-birthday present?"

"A present given when it isn't your birthday, of course."

Alice considered a little. "I like birthday presents best," she said at last.

"You don't know what you're talking about!" cried Humpty Dumpty. "How many days are there in a year?"

"Three hundred and sixty-five," said Alice.

"And how many birthdays have you?"

"One."

"And if you take one from three hundred and sixty-five, what remains?"

"Three hundred and sixty-four, of course."

Humpty Dumpty looked doubtful. "I'd rather see that done on paper," he said.

Alice couldn't help smiling as she took out her memorandum-book and worked the sum for him:

$$\begin{array}{r} 3\ 6\ 5 \\ 1 \\ \hline 3\ 6\ 4 \end{array}$$

Humpty Dumpty took the book and looked at it carefully. "That seems to be done right—" he began.

"You're holding it upside down!" Alice interrupted.

"To be sure I was!" Humpty Dumpty said gaily, as she turned it round for him. "I thought it looked a little queer. As I was saying, that *seems* to be done right—though I haven't time to look it over thoroughly just now—and that shows that there are three hundred and sixty-four days when you might get un-birthday presents——"

"Certainly," said Alice.

"And only *one* for birthday presents, you know. There's glory for you!"

"I don't know what you mean by 'glory,' " Alice said.

Humpty Dumpty smiled contemptuously. "Of course you don't—till I tell you. I meant 'there's a nice knock-down argument for you!' "

[102]

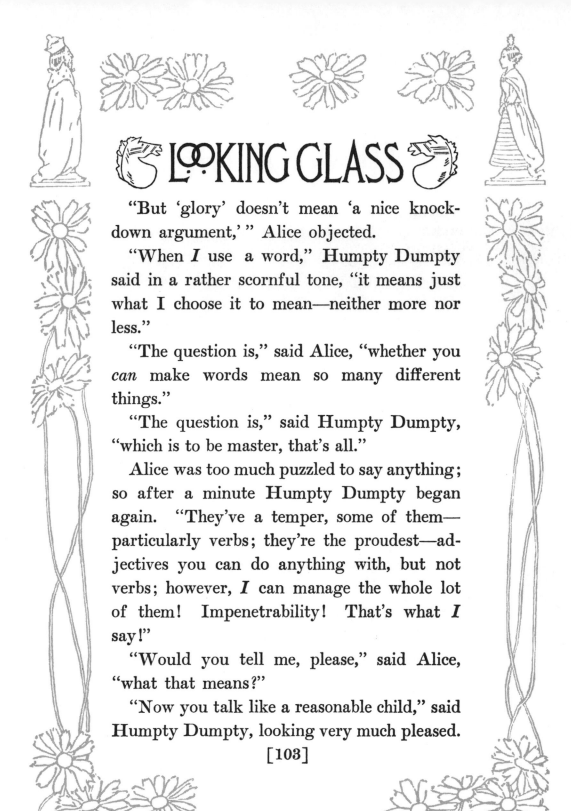

"But 'glory' doesn't mean 'a nice knock-down argument,'" Alice objected.

"When *I* use a word," Humpty Dumpty said in a rather scornful tone, "it means just what I choose it to mean—neither more nor less."

"The question is," said Alice, "whether you *can* make words mean so many different things."

"The question is," said Humpty Dumpty, "which is to be master, that's all."

Alice was too much puzzled to say anything; so after a minute Humpty Dumpty began again. "They've a temper, some of them—particularly verbs; they're the proudest—adjectives you can do anything with, but not verbs; however, *I* can manage the whole lot of them! Impenetrability! That's what *I* say!"

"Would you tell me, please," said Alice, "what that means?"

"Now you talk like a reasonable child," said Humpty Dumpty, looking very much pleased.

[103]

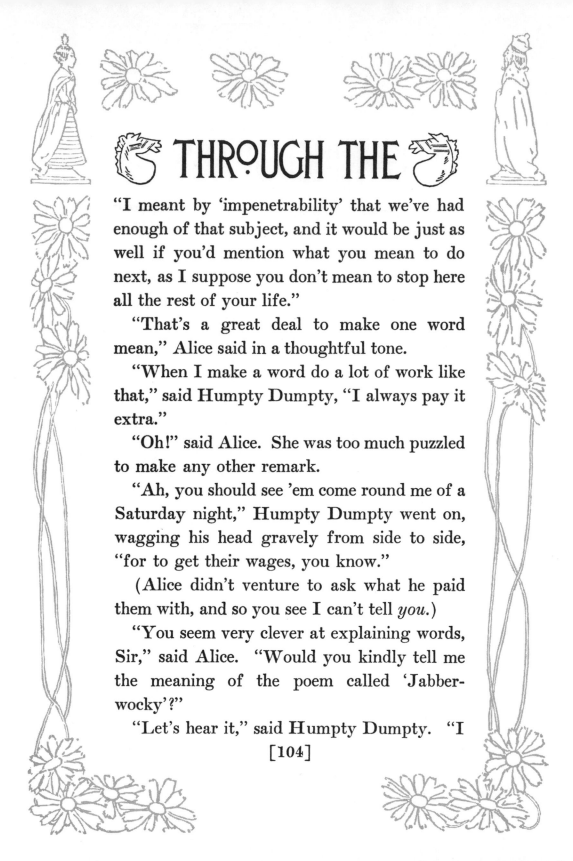

"I meant by 'impenetrability' that we've had enough of that subject, and it would be just as well if you'd mention what you mean to do next, as I suppose you don't mean to stop here all the rest of your life."

"That's a great deal to make one word mean," Alice said in a thoughtful tone.

"When I make a word do a lot of work like that," said Humpty Dumpty, "I always pay it extra."

"Oh!" said Alice. She was too much puzzled to make any other remark.

"Ah, you should see 'em come round me of a Saturday night," Humpty Dumpty went on, wagging his head gravely from side to side, "for to get their wages, you know."

(Alice didn't venture to ask what he paid them with, and so you see I can't tell *you*.)

"You seem very clever at explaining words, Sir," said Alice. "Would you kindly tell me the meaning of the poem called 'Jabberwocky'?"

"Let's hear it," said Humpty Dumpty. "I

[104]

can explain all the poems that ever were invented—and a good many that haven't been
invented just yet."

This sounded very hopeful, so Alice repeated
the first verse:

> " *'Twas brillig, and the slithy toves*
>   *Did gyre and gimble in the wabe:*
> *All mimsy were the borogoves,*
>   *And the mome raths outgrabe.*"

"That's enough to begin with," Humpty
Dumpty interrupted; "there are plenty of hard
words there. *'Brillig'* means four o'clock in
the afternoon—the time when you begin *broil-
ing* things for dinner."

"That'll do very well," said Alice; "and
'slithy'?"

"Well, *'slithy'* means 'lithe and slimy.'
'Lithe' is the same as 'active.' You see it's like
a portmanteau—there are two meanings
packed up into one word."

"I see it now," Alice remarked thoughtfully;
"and what are *'toves'*?"

[105]

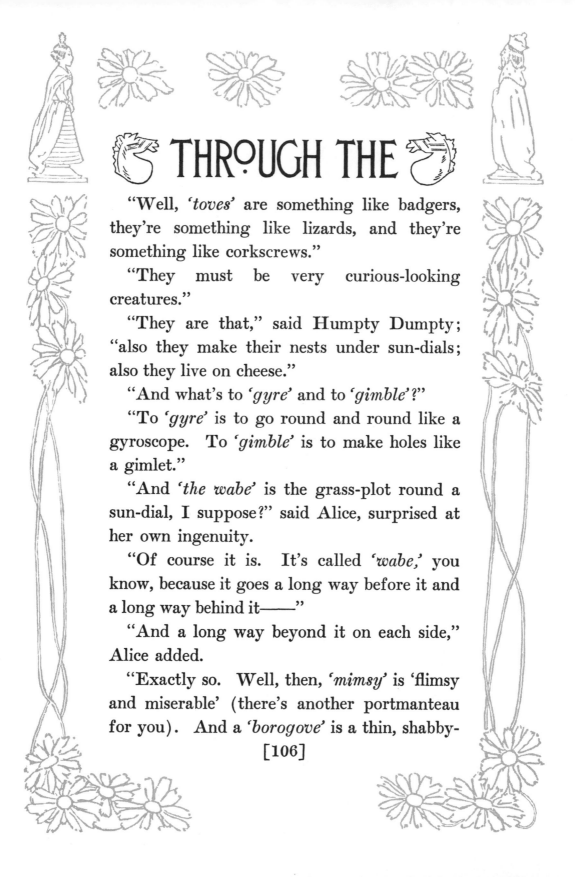

"Well, *'toves'* are something like badgers, they're something like lizards, and they're something like corkscrews."

"They must be very curious-looking creatures."

"They are that," said Humpty Dumpty; "also they make their nests under sun-dials; also they live on cheese."

"And what's to *'gyre'* and to *'gimble'*?"

"To *'gyre'* is to go round and round like a gyroscope. To *'gimble'* is to make holes like a gimlet."

"And *'the wabe'* is the grass-plot round a sun-dial, I suppose?" said Alice, surprised at her own ingenuity.

"Of course it is. It's called *'wabe,'* you know, because it goes a long way before it and a long way behind it——"

"And a long way beyond it on each side," Alice added.

"Exactly so. Well, then, *'mimsy'* is 'flimsy and miserable' (there's another portmanteau for you). And a *'borogove'* is a thin, shabby-

[106]

looking bird with its feathers sticking out all round—something like a live mop."

"And then *'mome raths'*?" said Alice. "I'm afraid I'm giving you a great deal of trouble."

"Well, a *'rath'* is a sort of green pig; but *'mome'* I'm not certain about. I think it's short for 'from home'—meaning that they'd lost their way, you know."

"And what does *'outgrabe'* mean?"

"Well, *'outgribing'* is something between bellowing and whistling, with a kind of sneeze in the middle; however, you'll hear it done, maybe, down in the wood yonder, and when you've once heard it you'll be *quite* content. Who's been repeating all that hard stuff to you?"

"I read it in a book," said Alice. "But I *had* some poetry repeated to me much easier than that by—Tweedledee, I think it was."

"As to poetry, you know," said Humpty Dumpty, stretching out one of his great hands, "*I* can repeat poetry as well as other folk, if it comes to that——"

[107]

"Oh, it needn't come to that!" Alice hastily said, hoping to keep him from beginning.

"The piece I'm going to repeat," he went on without noticing her remark, "was written entirely for your amusement."

Alice felt that in that case she really *ought* to listen to it, so she sat down and said "Thank you" rather sadly.

> *"In winter, when the fields are white,*
> *I sing this song for your delight——*

only I don't sing it," he added as an explanation.

"I see you don't," said Alice.

"If you can *see* whether I'm singing or not, you've sharper eyes than most," Humpty Dumpty remarked severely. Alice was silent.

> *"In spring, when woods are getting green,*
> *I'll try and tell you what I mean:"*

"Thank you very much," said Alice.

> *"In summer, when the days are long,*
> *Perhaps you'll understand the song:*

LOOKING GLASS

> *"In autumn, when the leaves are brown,*
> *Take pen and ink, and write it down."*

"I will, if I can remember it so long," said Alice.

"You needn't go on making remarks like that," Humpty Dumpty said; "they're not sensible and they put me out."

> *"I sent a message to the fish:*
> *I told them 'This is what I wish.'*

> *"The little fishes of the sea,*
> *They sent an answer back to me.*

> *"The little fishes' answer was*
> *'We cannot do it, Sir, because——'"*

"I'm afraid I don't quite understand," said Alice.

"It gets easier further on," Humpty Dumpty replied.

> *"I sent to them again to say*
> *'It will be better to obey.'*

> *"The fishes answered, with a grin,*
> *'Why, what a temper you are in!'*

[109]

THROUGH THE

"I told them once, I told them twice:
They would not listen to advice.

"I took a kettle large and new,
Fit for the deed I had to do.

"My heart went hop, my heart went thump:
I filled the kettle at the pump.

"Then some one came to me and said
'The little fishes are in bed.'

"I said to him, I said it plain,
'Then you must wake them up again.'

"I said it very loud and clear:
I went and shouted in his ear."

Humpty Dumpty raised his voice almost to
a scream as he repeated this verse, and Alice
thought, with a shudder, "I wouldn't have been
the messenger for *anything!*"

"But he was very stiff and proud:
He said 'You needn't shout so loud!'

"And he was very proud and stiff:
He said 'I'd go and wake them, if——'

[110]

"They must be very curious-looking creatures."

Page 106

"I said it very loud and clear:
I went and shouted in his ear."

Page 110

LOOKING GLASS

"I took a corkscrew from the shelf:
I went to wake them up myself.

"And when I found the door was locked,
I pulled and pushed and kicked and knocked.

"And when I found the door was shut,
I tried to turn the handle, but——"

There was a long pause.

"Is that all?" Alice timidly asked.

"That's all," said Humpty Dumpty. "Good-bye."

This was rather sudden, Alice thought; but after such a *very* strong hint that she ought to be going, she felt that it would hardly be civil to stay. So she got up and held out her hand. "Good-bye till we meet again!" she said as cheerfully as she could.

"I shouldn't know you again if we *did* meet," Humpty Dumpty replied in a discontented tone, giving her one of his fingers to shake; "you're so exactly like other people."

"The face is what one goes by, generally," Alice remarked in a thoughtful tone.

[111]

"That's just what I complain of," said Humpty Dumpty. "Your face is the same as everybody has—the two eyes, so—" (marking their places in the air with his thumb) "nose in the middle, mouth under. It's always the same. Now if you had the two eyes on the same side of the nose, for instance, or the mouth at the top, that would be *some* help."

"It wouldn't look nice," Alice objected. But Humpty Dumpty only shut his eyes and said, "Wait till you've tried."

Alice waited a minute to see if he would speak again, but as he never opened his eyes or took any further notice of her, she said "Good-bye!" once more, and getting no answer to this, she quietly walked away; but she couldn't help saying to herself as she went, "Of all the unsatisfactory—" (she repeated this aloud, as it was a great comfort to have such a long word to say) "of all the unsatisfactory people I *ever* met—" She never finished the sentence, for at this moment a heavy crash shook the forest from end to end.

[112]

THE LION AND THE UNICORN

THE next moment soldiers came running through the wood, at first in twos and threes, then ten or twenty together, and at last in such crowds that they seemed to fill the whole forest. Alice got behind a tree, for fear of being run over, and watched them go by.

She thought that in all her life she had never seen soldiers so uncertain on their feet; they were always tripping over something or other, and whenever one went down, several more always fell over him, so that the ground was soon covered with little heaps of men.

Then came the horses. Having four feet, these managed rather better than the foot-soldiers; but even *they* stumbled now and then; and it seemed to be a regular rule that whenever a horse stumbled the rider fell off in-

stantly. The confusion got worse every moment, and Alice was very glad to get out of the wood into an open place, where she found the White King seated on the ground busily writing in his memorandum-book.

"I've sent them all!" the King cried in a tone of delight on seeing Alice. "Did you happen to meet any soldiers, my dear, as you came through the wood?"

"Yes, I did," said Alice; "several thousand, I should think."

"Four thousand two hundred and seven, that's the exact number," the King said, referring to his book. "I couldn't send all the horses, you know, because two of them are wanted in the game. And I haven't sent the two Messengers, either. They're both gone to the town. Just look along the road and tell me if you can see either of them."

"I see nobody on the road," said Alice.

"I only wish *I* had such eyes," the King remarked in a fretful tone. "To be able to see Nobody! And at that distance, too! Why,

[114]

# LOOKING GLASS

it's as much as *I* can do to see real people by
this light!"

All this was lost on Alice, who was still looking intently along the road, shading her eyes
with one hand. "I see somebody now!" she
exclaimed at last. "But he's coming very
slowly, and what curious attitudes he goes
into!" (For the Messenger kept skipping up
and down and wriggling like an eel as he came
along, with his great hands spread out like
fans on each side.)

"Not at all," said the King. "He's an
Anglo-Saxon Messenger, and those are Anglo-
Saxon attitudes. He only does them when he's
happy. His name is Haigha." (He pro-
nounced it so as to rhyme with "mayor.")

"I love my love with an **H**," Alice couldn't
help beginning, "because he is Happy. I hate
him with an **H**, because he is Hideous. I fed
him with—with—with Ham-sandwiches and
Hay. His name is Haigha, and he lives——"

"He lives on the Hill," the King remarked
simply, without the least idea that he was join-

[115]

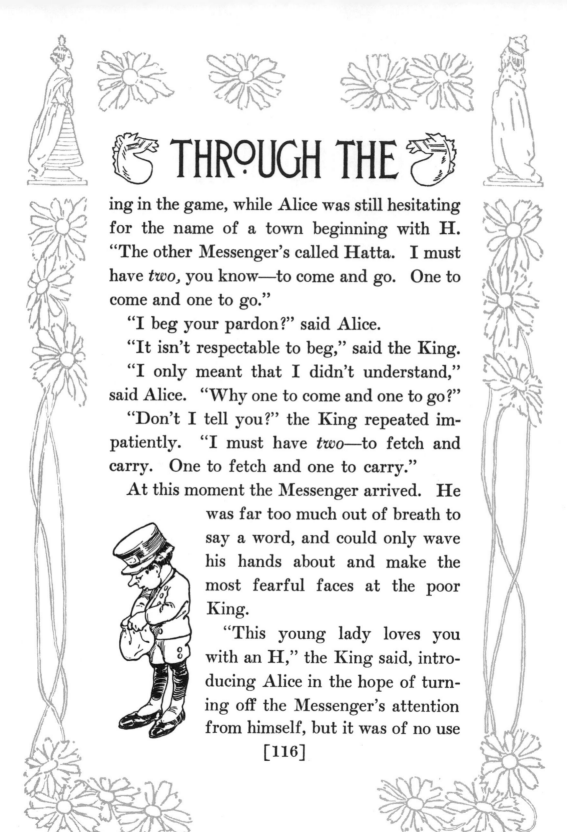

ing in the game, while Alice was still hesitating for the name of a town beginning with H. "The other Messenger's called Hatta. I must have *two,* you know—to come and go. One to come and one to go."

"I beg your pardon?" said Alice.

"It isn't respectable to beg," said the King.

"I only meant that I didn't understand," said Alice. "Why one to come and one to go?"

"Don't I tell you?" the King repeated impatiently. "I must have *two*—to fetch and carry. One to fetch and one to carry."

At this moment the Messenger arrived. He was far too much out of breath to say a word, and could only wave his hands about and make the most fearful faces at the poor King.

"This young lady loves you with an H," the King said, introducing Alice in the hope of turning off the Messenger's attention from himself, but it was of no use

[116]

 LOOKING GLASS

—the Anglo-Saxon attitudes only got more extraordinary every moment, while the great eyes rolled wildly from side to side.

"You alarm me!" said the King. "I feel faint. Give me a ham sandwich!"

On which the Messenger, to Alice's great amusement, opened a bag that hung round his neck and handed a sandwich to the King, who devoured it greedily.

"Another sandwich!" said the King.

"There's nothing but hay left now," the Messenger said, peeping into the bag.

"Hay, then," the King murmured in a faint whisper.

Alice was glad to see that it revived him a good deal. "There's nothing like eating hay when you're faint," he remarked to her, as he munched away.

"I should think throwing cold water over you would be better," Alice suggested; "or some sal-volatile."

"I didn't say there was nothing *better*," the King replied. "I said there was nothing *like* it." Which Alice did not venture to deny.

[117]

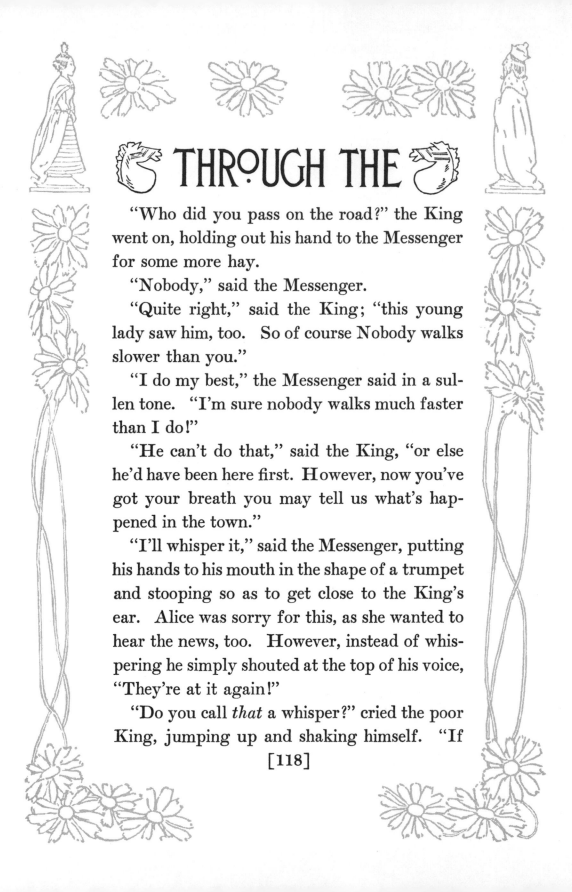

"Who did you pass on the road?" the King went on, holding out his hand to the Messenger for some more hay.

"Nobody," said the Messenger.

"Quite right," said the King; "this young lady saw him, too. So of course Nobody walks slower than you."

"I do my best," the Messenger said in a sullen tone. "I'm sure nobody walks much faster than I do!"

"He can't do that," said the King, "or else he'd have been here first. However, now you've got your breath you may tell us what's happened in the town."

"I'll whisper it," said the Messenger, putting his hands to his mouth in the shape of a trumpet and stooping so as to get close to the King's ear. Alice was sorry for this, as she wanted to hear the news, too. However, instead of whispering he simply shouted at the top of his voice, "They're at it again!"

"Do you call *that* a whisper?" cried the poor King, jumping up and shaking himself. "If

LOOKING GLASS

you do such a thing again I'll have you buttered! It went through and through my head
like an earthquake!"

"It would have to be a very tiny earthquake!" thought Alice. "Who are at it again?"
she ventured to ask.

"Why, the Lion and the Unicorn, of
course," said the King.

"Fighting for the crown?"

"Yes, to be sure," said the King; "and the
best of the joke is, that it's *my* crown all the
while! Let's run and see them." And they
trotted off, Alice repeating to herself as she
ran the words of the old song:

"The Lion and the Unicorn were fighting for the
crown:
The Lion beat the Unicorn all round the town.
Some gave them white bread, some gave them brown:
Some gave them plum-cake and drummed them out
of town."

"Does—the one—that wins—get the crown?"
she asked as well as she could, for the run was
putting her quite out of breath.

"Dear me, no!" said the King. "What an idea!"

"Would you—be good enough—" Alice panted out, after running a little further, "to stop a minute—just to get—one's breath again?"

"I'm *good* enough," the King said, "only I'm not *strong* enough. You see, a minute goes by so fearfully quick. You might as well try to stop a Bandersnatch!"

Alice had no more breath for talking, so they trotted on in silence till they came into sight of a great crowd, in the middle of which

the Lion and Unicorn were fighting. They were in such a cloud of dust that at first Alice could not make out which was which; but she soon managed to distinguish the Unicorn by his horn.

They placed themselves close to where Hatta, the other Messenger, was standing watching

[120]

the fight, with a cup of tea in one hand and a piece of bread-and-butter in the other.

"He's only just out of prison, and he hadn't finished his tea when he was sent in," Haigha whispered to Alice; "and they only give them oyster-shells in there, so you see he's very hungry and thirsty. How are you, dear child?" he went on, putting his arm affectionately round Hatta's neck.

Hatta looked round and nodded, and went on with his bread-and-butter.

"Were you happy in prison, dear child?" said Haigha.

Hatta looked round once more, and this time a tear or two trickled down his cheek; but not a word would he say.

"Speak, can't you!" Haigha cried impatiently. But Hatta only munched away and drank some more tea.

"Speak, won't you!" cried the King. "How are they getting on with the fight?"

Hatta made a desperate effort, and swallowed a large piece of bread-and-butter.

[121]

"They're getting on very well," he said in a choking voice; "each of them has been down about eighty-seven times."

"Then I suppose they'll soon bring the white bread and the brown?" Alice ventured to remark.

"It's waiting for 'em now," said Hatta; "this is a bit of it as I'm eating."

There was a pause in the fight just then, and the Lion and the Unicorn sat down, panting, while the King called out, "Ten minutes allowed for refreshments!" Haigha and Hatta set to work at once, carrying round trays of white and brown bread. Alice took a piece to taste, but it was *very* dry.

"I don't think they'll fight any more today," the King said to Hatta; "go and order the drums to begin." And Hatta went bounding away like a grasshopper.

For a minute or two Alice stood silent, watching him. Suddenly she brightened up. "Look, look!" she cried, pointing eagerly. "There's the White Queen running across the

LOOKING GLASS

country! She came flying out of the wood over yonder. How fast those Queens *can* run!"

"There's some enemy after her, no doubt," the King said, without even looking round. "That wood's full of them."

"But aren't you going to run and help her?" Alice asked, very much surprised at his taking it so quietly.

"No use, no use!" said the King. "She runs so fearfully quick. You might as well try to catch a Bandersnatch! But I'll make a memorandum about her, if you like. She's a dear, good creature," he repeated softly to himself as he opened his memorandum-book. "Do you spell 'creature' with a double 'e'?"

At this moment the Unicorn sauntered by them with his hands in his pockets. "I had the best of it this time," he said to the King, just glancing at him as he passed.

"A little—a little," the King replied, rather nervously. "You shouldn't have run him through with your horn, you know."

"It didn't hurt him," the Unicorn said care-

[123]

lessly, and he was going on, when his eye happened to fall upon Alice. He turned round instantly, and stood for some time looking at her with an air of the deepest disgust.

"What—is—this?" he said at last.

"This is a child!" Haigha replied eagerly, coming in front of Alice to introduce her, and spreading out both his hands towards her in an Anglo-Saxon attitude. "We only found it to-day. It's as large as life, and twice as natural!"

"I always thought they were fabulous monsters!" said the Unicorn. "Is it alive?"

"It can talk," said Haigha solemnly.

The Unicorn looked dreamily at Alice and said, "Talk, child."

Alice could not help her lips curling up into a smile as she began: "Do you know, I always thought Unicorns were fabulous monsters, too? I never saw one alive before!"

"Well, now that we *have* seen each other," said the Unicorn, "if you'll believe in me, I'll believe in you. Is that a bargain?"

[124]

"Yes, if you like," said Alice.

"Come, fetch out the plum-cake, old man!" the Unicorn went on, turning from her to the King. "None of your brown bread for me!"

"Certainly—certainly!" the King muttered, and beckoned to Haigha. "Open the bag!" he whispered. "Quick! Not that one—that's full of hay!"

Haigha took a large cake out of the bag and gave it to Alice to hold while he got out a dish and carving-knife. How they all came out of it Alice couldn't guess. It was just like a conjuring-trick, she thought.

The Lion had joined them while this was going on. He looked very tired and sleepy, and his eyes were half shut. "What's this!" he said, blinking lazily at Alice, and speaking in a deep, hollow tone that sounded like the tolling of a great bell.

"Ah, what *is* it, now?" the Unicorn cried eagerly. "You'll never guess! *I* couldn't."

The Lion looked at Alice wearily. "Are you

[125]

animal—or vegetable—or mineral?" he said, yawning at every other word.

"It's a fabulous monster!" the Unicorn cried out before Alice could reply.

"Then hand round the plum-cake, Monster," the Lion said, lying down and putting his chin on his paws. "And sit down, both of you" (to the King and the Unicorn); "fair play with the cake, you know!"

The King was evidently very uncomfortable at having to sit down between the two great creatures; but there was no other place for him.

"What a fight we might have for the crown *now!*" the Unicorn said, looking slyly up at the crown, which the poor King was nearly shaking off his head, he trembled so much.

"I should win easy," said the Lion.

"I'm not so sure of that," said the Unicorn.

"Why, I beat you all round the town, you chicken!" the Lion replied angrily, half getting up as he spoke.

Here the King interrupted to prevent the quarrel going on; he was very nervous, and his

[126]

"Are you animal—or vegetable—or mineral?"

Page 125

"If *that* doesn't 'drum them out of town,'
nothing ever will!"

Page 128

Humpty Dumpty took the book,
and looked at it carefully.

Page 102

"You're my prisoner!" the Knight cried.

Page 130

voice quite quivered. "All round the town?" he said. "That's a good long way. Did you go by the old bridge or the market-place? You get the best view by the old bridge."

"I'm sure I don't know," the Lion growled out as he lay down again. "There was too much dust to see anything. What a time the Monster is cutting up that cake!"

Alice had seated herself on the bank of a little brook, with the great dish on her knees, and was sawing away diligently with the knife. "It's very provoking!" she said in reply to the Lion (she was getting quite used to being called "the Monster"). "I've cut several slices already, but they always join on again!"

"You don't know how to manage Looking-glass cakes," the Unicorn remarked. "Hand it round first and cut it afterwards."

This sounded nonsense, but Alice very obediently got up and carried the dish round, and the cake divided itself into three pieces as she did so. "*Now* cut it up," said the Lion, as she returned to her place with the empty dish.

[127]

"I say, this isn't fair!" cried the Unicorn, as Alice sat with the knife in her hand, very much puzzled how to begin. "The Monster has given the Lion twice as much as me!"

"She's kept none for herself, anyhow," said the Lion. "Do you like plum-cake, Monster?"

But before Alice could answer him the drums began.

Where the noise came from she couldn't make out; the air seemed full of it, and it rang through and through her head till she felt quite deafened. She started to her feet and sprang across the little brook in her terror,

* * * * * *

* * * * *

* * * * * *

and had just time to see the Lion and the Unicorn rise to their feet, with angry looks at being interrupted in their feast, before she dropped to her knees and put her hands over her ears, vainly trying to shut out the dreadful uproar.

"If *that* doesn't 'drum them out of town,'" she thought to herself, "nothing ever will!"

[128]

LOOKING GLASS

"IT'S MY OWN INVENTION"

AFTER a while the noise seemed grad-
ually to die away, till all was dead
silence, and Alice lifted up her head
in some alarm. There was no one to be seen,
and her first thought was that she must have
been dreaming about the Lion and the Unicorn
and those queer Anglo-Saxon Messengers.
However, there was the great dish still lying
at her feet on which she had tried to cut the
plum-cake. "So I wasn't dreaming, after all,"
she said to herself, "unless—unless we're all
part of the same dream. Only I do hope it's
my dream and not the Red King's! I don't
like belonging to another person's dream," she
went on in a rather complaining tone. "I've a
great mind to go and wake him and see what
happens!"

At this moment her thoughts were inter-

rupted by a loud shouting of "Ahoy! Ahoy! Check!" and a Knight, dressed in crimson armor, came galloping down upon her, brandishing a great club. Just as he reached her the horse stopped suddenly. "You're my prisoner!" the Knight cried as he tumbled off his horse.

Startled as she was, Alice was more frightened for him than for herself at the moment, and watched him with some anxiety as he mounted again. As soon as he was comfortably in the saddle, he began once more, "You're my—" but here another voice broke in, "Ahoy! Ahoy! Check!" and Alice looked round in some surprise for the new enemy.

This time it was a White Knight. He drew up at Alice's side, and tumbled off his horse just as the Red Knight had done; then he got on again, and the two Knights sat and looked at each other for some time without speaking. Alice looked from one to the other in some bewilderment.

[130]

LOOKING GLASS

"She's *my* prisoner, you know!" the Red Knight said at last.

"Yes, but then *I* came and rescued her!" the White Knight replied.

"Well, we must fight for her, then," said the Red Knight, as he took up his helmet (which hung from the saddle, and was something the shape of a horse's head) and put it on.

"You will observe the Rules of Battle, of course?" the White Knight remarked, putting on his helmet, too.

"I always do," said the Red Knight, and they began banging away at each other with such fury that Alice got behind a tree to be out of the way of the blows.

"I wonder, now, what the Rules of Battle

are," she said to herself, as she watched the fight, timidly peeping out from her hiding-place. "One Rule seems to be that if one Knight hits the other, he knocks him off his horse; and if he misses he tumbles off himself; and another Rule seems to be that they hold their clubs with their arms, as if they were Punch and Judy. What a noise they make when they tumble! Just like a whole set of fire-irons falling into the fender! And how quiet the horses are! They let them get on and off them just as if they were tables!"

Another Rule of Battle, that Alice had not noticed, seemed to be that they always fell on their heads; and the battle ended with their both falling off in this way, side by side. When they got up again they shook hands, and then the Red Knight mounted and galloped off.

"It was a glorious victory, wasn't it?" said the White Knight as he came up panting.

"I don't know," Alice said doubtfully. "I don't want to be anybody's prisoner. I want to be a Queen."

[132]

LOOKING GLASS

"So you will when you've crossed the next brook," said the White Knight. "I'll see you safe to the end of the wood—and then I must go back, you know. That's the end of my move."

"Thank you very much," said Alice. "May I help you off with your helmet?" It was evidently more than he could manage by himself; however, she managed to shake him out of it at last.

"Now one can breathe more easily," said the Knight, putting back his shaggy hair with both hands and turning his gentle face and large mild eyes to Alice. She thought she had never seen such a strange-looking soldier in all her life.

He was dressed in tin armor, which seemed to fit him very badly, and he had a queer-shaped little deal box fastened across his shoulders, upside-down, and with the lid hanging open. Alice looked at it with great curiosity.

"I see you're admiring my little box," the Knight said in a friendly tone. "It's my own

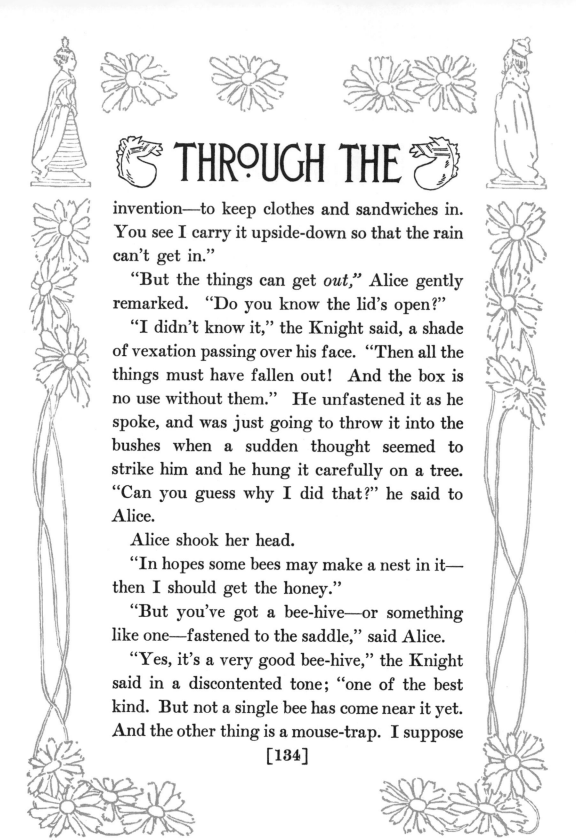

invention—to keep clothes and sandwiches in. You see I carry it upside-down so that the rain can't get in."

"But the things can get *out*," Alice gently remarked. "Do you know the lid's open?"

"I didn't know it," the Knight said, a shade of vexation passing over his face. "Then all the things must have fallen out! And the box is no use without them." He unfastened it as he spoke, and was just going to throw it into the bushes when a sudden thought seemed to strike him and he hung it carefully on a tree. "Can you guess why I did that?" he said to Alice.

Alice shook her head.

"In hopes some bees may make a nest in it— then I should get the honey."

"But you've got a bee-hive—or something like one—fastened to the saddle," said Alice.

"Yes, it's a very good bee-hive," the Knight said in a discontented tone; "one of the best kind. But not a single bee has come near it yet. And the other thing is a mouse-trap. I suppose

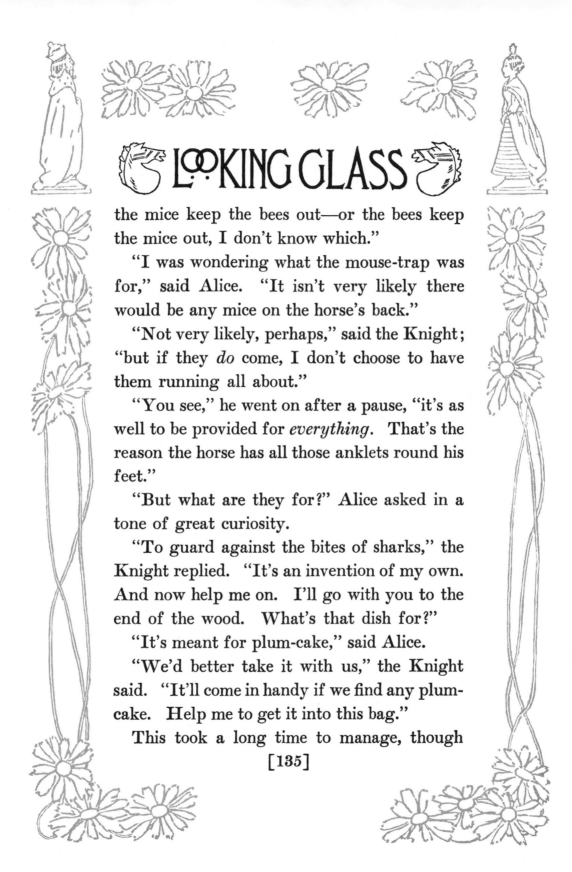

the mice keep the bees out—or the bees keep the mice out, I don't know which."

"I was wondering what the mouse-trap was for," said Alice. "It isn't very likely there would be any mice on the horse's back."

"Not very likely, perhaps," said the Knight; "but if they *do* come, I don't choose to have them running all about."

"You see," he went on after a pause, "it's as well to be provided for *everything*. That's the reason the horse has all those anklets round his feet."

"But what are they for?" Alice asked in a tone of great curiosity.

"To guard against the bites of sharks," the Knight replied. "It's an invention of my own. And now help me on. I'll go with you to the end of the wood. What's that dish for?"

"It's meant for plum-cake," said Alice.

"We'd better take it with us," the Knight said. "It'll come in handy if we find any plum-cake. Help me to get it into this bag."

This took a long time to manage, though

THROUGH THE

Alice held the bag open very carefully, because the Knight was so *very* awkward in putting in the dish; the first two or three times that he tried he fell in himself instead. "It's rather a tight fit, you see," he said, as they got it in at last; "there are so many candlesticks in the bag." And he hung it to the saddle, which was already loaded with bunches of carrots and fire-irons and many other things.

"I hope you've got your hair well fastened on?" he continued, as they set off.

"Only in the usual way," Alice said, smiling.

"That's hardly enough," he said, anxiously. "You see the wind is so *very* strong here. It's as strong as soup."

"Have you invented a plan for keeping the hair from being blown off?" Alice inquired.

"Not yet," said the Knight. "But I've got a plan for keeping it from *falling* off."

"I should like to hear it very much."

"First you take an upright stick," said the Knight. "Then you make your hair creep up it, like a fruit-tree. Now, the reason hair falls

[136]

"They hold their clubs with their arms,
as if they were Punch and Judy."

Page 132

The poor Knight was certainly not a good rider.

Page 137

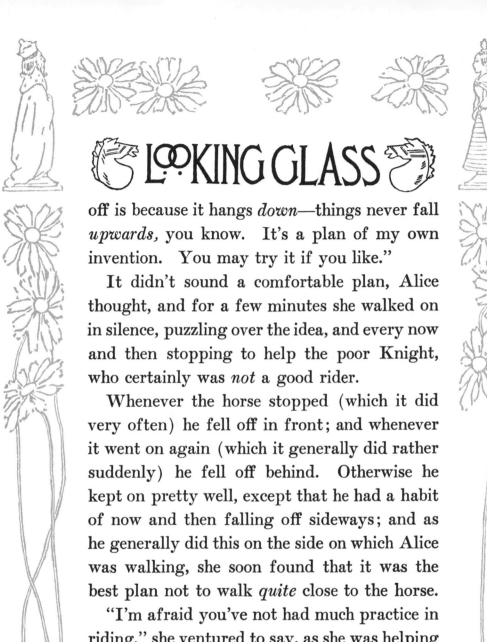

off is because it hangs *down*—things never fall *upwards,* you know. It's a plan of my own invention. You may try it if you like."

It didn't sound a comfortable plan, Alice thought, and for a few minutes she walked on in silence, puzzling over the idea, and every now and then stopping to help the poor Knight, who certainly was *not* a good rider.

Whenever the horse stopped (which it did very often) he fell off in front; and whenever it went on again (which it generally did rather suddenly) he fell off behind. Otherwise he kept on pretty well, except that he had a habit of now and then falling off sideways; and as he generally did this on the side on which Alice was walking, she soon found that it was the best plan not to walk *quite* close to the horse.

"I'm afraid you've not had much practice in riding," she ventured to say, as she was helping him up from his fifth tumble.

The Knight looked very much surprised and a little offended at the remark. "What makes you say that?" he asked, as he scrambled back

[137]

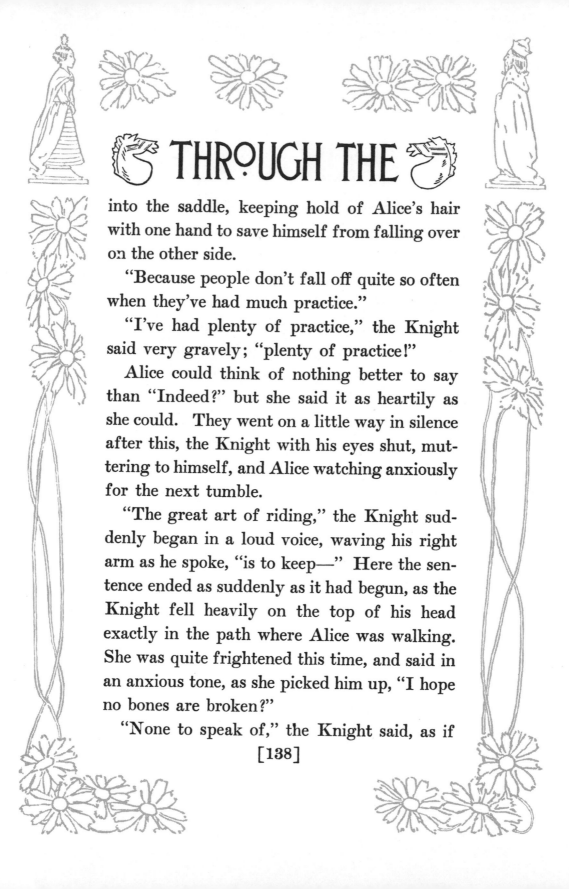

into the saddle, keeping hold of Alice's hair with one hand to save himself from falling over on the other side.

"Because people don't fall off quite so often when they've had much practice."

"I've had plenty of practice," the Knight said very gravely; "plenty of practice!"

Alice could think of nothing better to say than "Indeed?" but she said it as heartily as she could. They went on a little way in silence after this, the Knight with his eyes shut, muttering to himself, and Alice watching anxiously for the next tumble.

"The great art of riding," the Knight suddenly began in a loud voice, waving his right arm as he spoke, "is to keep—" Here the sentence ended as suddenly as it had begun, as the Knight fell heavily on the top of his head exactly in the path where Alice was walking. She was quite frightened this time, and said in an anxious tone, as she picked him up, "I hope no bones are broken?"

"None to speak of," the Knight said, as if

he didn't mind breaking two or three of them.
"The great art of riding, as I was saying, is—
to keep your balance properly. Like this, you
know——"

He let go the bridle and stretched out both
his arms to show Alice what he meant, and this
time he fell flat on his back right under the
horse's feet.

"Plenty of practice!" he went on repeating
all the time that Alice was getting him on his
feet again. "Plenty of practice!"

"It's too ridiculous!" cried Alice, losing all
her patience this time. "You ought to have a
wooden horse on wheels, that you ought!"

"Does that kind go smoothly?" the Knight
asked in a tone of great interest, clasping his
arms round the horse's neck as he spoke, just in
time to save himself from tumbling off again.

"Much more smoothly than a live horse,"
Alice said, with a little scream of laughter, in
spite of all she could do to prevent it.

"I'll get one," the Knight said thoughtfully
to himself. "One or two—several."

There was a short silence after this, and then the Knight went on again. "I'm a great hand at inventing things. Now, I daresay you noticed, the last time you picked me up, that I was looking rather thoughtful?"

"You *were* a little grave," said Alice.

"Well, just then I was inventing a new way of getting over a gate. Would you like to hear it?"

"Very much indeed," Alice said politely.

"I'll tell you how I came to think of it," said the Knight. "You see, I said to myself, 'The only difficulty is with the feet; the *head* is high enough already.' Now, first I put my head on the top of the gate—then the head's high enough; then I stand on my head—then the feet are high enough, you see; then I'm over, you see."

"Yes, I suppose you'd be over when that was done," Alice said thoughtfully; "but don't you think it would be rather hard?"

"I haven't tried it yet," the Knight said

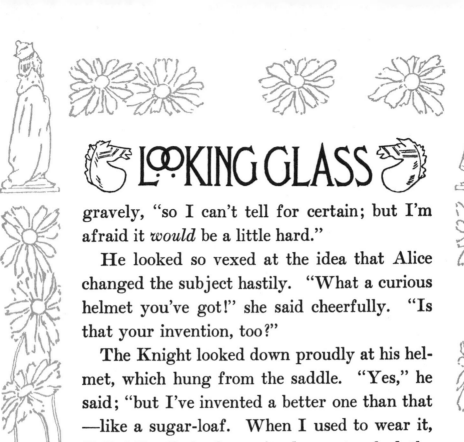

gravely, "so I can't tell for certain; but I'm afraid it *would* be a little hard."

He looked so vexed at the idea that Alice changed the subject hastily. "What a curious helmet you've got!" she said cheerfully. "Is that your invention, too?"

The Knight looked down proudly at his helmet, which hung from the saddle. "Yes," he said; "but I've invented a better one than that —like a sugar-loaf. When I used to wear it, if I fell off the horse it always touched the ground directly. So I had a *very* little way to fall, you see. But there *was* the danger of falling *into* it, to be sure. That happened to me once—and the worst of it was, before I could get out again the other White Knight came and put it on. He thought it was his own helmet."

The Knight looked so solemn about it that Alice did not dare to laugh. "I'm afraid you must have hurt him," she said in a trembling voice, "being on the top of his head."

"I had to kick him, of course," the Knight

[141]

said very seriously. "And then he took the helmet off again, but it took hours and hours to get me out. I was as fast as—as lightning, you know."

"But that's a different kind of fastness," Alice objected.

The Knight shook his head. "It was all kinds of fastness with me, I can assure you!" he said. He raised his hands in some excitement as he said this, and instantly rolled out of the saddle and fell headlong into a deep ditch.

Alice ran to the side of the ditch to look for him. She was rather startled by the fall, as for some time he had kept on very well, and she was afraid that he really *was* hurt this time. However, though she could see nothing but the soles of his feet, she was much relieved to hear that he was talking on in his usual tone. "All kinds of fastness," he repeated; "but it was careless of him to put another man's helmet on —with the man in it, too."

"How *can* you go on talking so quietly, head downwards?" Alice asked, as she dragged him

[142]

 LOOKING GLASS

out by the feet and laid him in a heap on the bank.

The Knight looked surprised at the question. "What does it matter where my body happens to be?" he said. "My mind goes on working all the same. In fact, the more head-downwards I am, the more I keep inventing new things."

"Now the cleverest thing of the sort that I ever did," he went on after a pause, "was inventing a new pudding during the meat-course."

"In time to have it cooked for the next course?" said Alice. "Well, that *was* quick work, certainly!"

"Well, not the *next* course," the Knight said in a slow, thoughtful tone; "no, certainly not the next *course*."

"Then it would have to be the next day. I suppose you wouldn't have two pudding-courses in one dinner?"

"Well, not the *next* day," the Knight repeated as before; "not the next *day*. In fact," he went on, holding his head down, and his voice getting lower and lower, "I don't believe

[143]

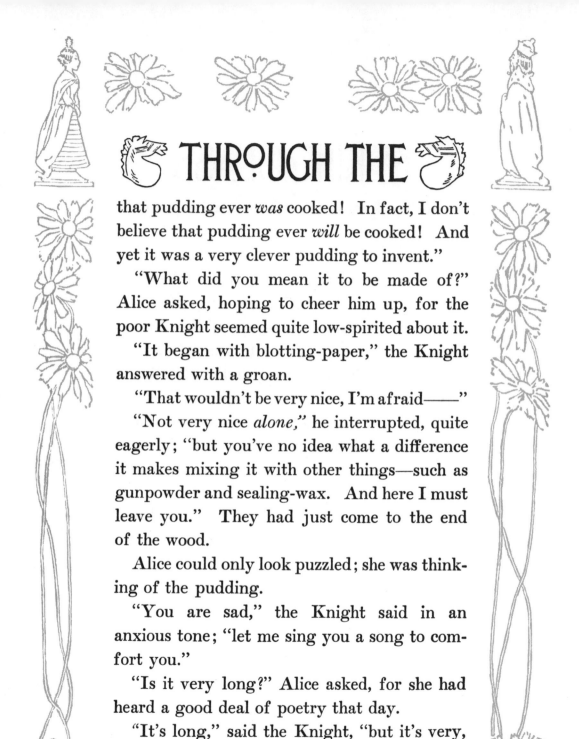

that pudding ever *was* cooked! In fact, I don't
believe that pudding ever *will* be cooked! And
yet it was a very clever pudding to invent."

"What did you mean it to be made of?"
Alice asked, hoping to cheer him up, for the
poor Knight seemed quite low-spirited about it.

"It began with blotting-paper," the Knight
answered with a groan.

"That wouldn't be very nice, I'm afraid——"

"Not very nice *alone*," he interrupted, quite
eagerly; "but you've no idea what a difference
it makes mixing it with other things—such as
gunpowder and sealing-wax. And here I must
leave you." They had just come to the end
of the wood.

Alice could only look puzzled; she was thinking of the pudding.

"You are sad," the Knight said in an
anxious tone; "let me sing you a song to comfort you."

"Is it very long?" Alice asked, for she had
heard a good deal of poetry that day.

"It's long," said the Knight, "but it's very,

  LOOKING GLASS

very beautiful. Everybody that hears me sing it—either it brings the *tears* into their eyes, or else——"

"Or else what?" said Alice, for the Knight had made a sudden pause.

"Or else it doesn't, you know. The name of the song is called '*Haddocks' Eyes.*'"

"Oh, that's the name of the song, is it?" Alice said, trying to feel interested.

"No, you don't understand," the Knight said, looking a little vexed. "That's what the name is *called*. The name really *is* '*The Aged Aged Man.*'"

"Then I ought to have said, 'That's what the *song* is called'?" Alice corrected herself.

"No, you oughtn't; that's quite another thing! The *song* is called '*Ways and Means*'; but that's only what it's *called,* you know!"

"Well, what *is* the song, then?" said Alice, who was by this time completely bewildered.

"I was coming to that," the Knight said. "The song really *is* '*A-sitting On A Gate,*' and the tune's my own invention."

So saying, he stopped his horse and let the reins fall on its neck; then, slowly beating time with one hand, and with a faint smile lighting up his gentle, foolish face, as if he enjoyed the music of his song, he began.

Of all the strange things that Alice saw in her journey Through the Looking-Glass, this was the one that she always remembered most clearly. Years afterwards she could bring the whole scene back again as if it had been only yesterday—the mild blue eyes and kindly smile of the Knight, the setting sun gleaming through his hair and shining on his armour in a blaze of light that quite dazzled her, the horse quietly moving about, with the reins hanging loose on his neck, cropping the grass at her feet, and the black shadows of the forest behind—all this she took in like a picture, as, with one hand shading her eyes, she leant against a tree, watching the strange pair, and listening in a half-dream to the melancholy music of the song.

"But the tune *isn't* his own invention," she

L⚇KING GLASS

said to herself; "it's *I give thee all, I can no more.*'" She stood and listened very attentively, but no tears came into her eyes.

> "*I'll tell thee everything I can:*
>   *There's little to relate.*
> *I saw an aged aged man*
>   *A-sitting on a gate.*
> '*Who are you, aged man?' I said.*
>   '*And how is it you live?'*
> *And his answer trickled through my head,*
>   *Like water through a sieve.*
>
> "*He said 'I look for butterflies*
>   *That sleep among the wheat:*
> *I make them into mutton-pies,*
>   *And sell them in the street.*
> *I sell them unto men,' he said,*
>   '*Who sail on stormy seas;*
> *And that's the way I get my bread—*
>   *A trifle, if you please.'*
>
> "*But I was thinking of a plan*
>   *To dye one's whiskers green,*
> *And always use so large a fan*
>   *That they could not be seen.*

# THROUGH THE

So, having no reply to give
To what the old man said,
I cried 'Come, tell me how you live!'
And thumped him on the head.

"His accents mild took up the tale:
He said 'I go my ways,
And when I find a mountain-rill,
I set it in a blaze;
And thence they make a stuff they call
Rowland's Macassar-Oil—
Yet twopence-halfpenny is all
They give me for my toil.'

"But I was thinking of a way
To feed oneself on batter,
And so go on from day to day
Getting a little fatter.
I shook him well from side to side,
Until his face was blue:
'Come, tell me how you live,' I cried,
'And what it is you do!'

"He said 'I hunt for haddocks' eyes
Among the heather bright,
And work them into waistcoat-buttons
In the silent night.

[148]

 LKING GLASS

And these I do not sell for gold
 Or coin of silvery shine,
But for a copper halfpenny,
 And that will purchase nine.

" 'I sometimes dig for buttered rolls,
 Or set limed twigs for crabs:
I sometimes search the grassy knolls
 For wheels of Hansom-cabs.
And that's the way' (he gave a wink)
 'By which I get my wealth—
And very gladly will I drink
 Your Honor's noble health.'

"I heard him then, for I had just
 Completed my design
To keep the Menai bridge from rust
 By boiling it in wine.
I thanked him much for telling me
 The way he got his wealth,
But chiefly for his wish that he
 Might drink my noble health.

"And now, if e'er by chance I put
 My fingers into glue,
Or madly squeeze a right-hand foot
 Into a left-hand shoe,

[149]

Or if I drop upon my toe
* A very heavy weight,*
I weep, for it reminds me so
Of that old man I used to know—
Whose look was mild, whose speech was slow,
Whose hair was whiter than the snow,
Whose face was very like a crow,
With eyes, like cinders, all aglow,
Who seemed distracted with his woe,
Who rocked his body to and fro,
And muttered mumblingly and low,
As if his mouth were full of dough,
Who snorted like a buffalo——
That summer evening long ago,
* A-sitting on a gate."*

As the Knight sang the last words of the ballad, he gathered up the reins and turned his horse's head along the road by which they had come. "You've only a few yards to go," he said, "down the hill and over that little brook, and then you'll be a Queen. But you'll stay and see me off first?" he added as Alice turned with an eager look in the direction to which he pointed. "I sha'n't be long. You'll

[150]

wait and wave your handkerchief when I get
to that turn in the road! I think it'll encourage
me, you see."

"Of course I'll wait," said Alice; "and thank
you very much for coming so far—and for the
song. I liked it very much."

"I hope so," the Knight said doubtfully;
"but you didn't cry so much as I thought you
would."

So they shook hands, and then the Knight
rode slowly away into the forest. "It won't
take long to see him *off*, I expect," Alice said
to herself as she stood watching him. "There
he goes! Right on his head as
usual! However, he gets on
again pretty easily; that comes
of having so many things hung
round the horse—" So she
went on talking to herself as
she watched the horse walking
leisurely along the road, and the
Knight tumbling off, first on one
side and then on the other. After

[151]

the fourth or fifth tumble he reached the turn, and then she waved her handkerchief to him, and waited till he was out of sight.

"I hope it encouraged him," she said as she turned to run down the hill; "and now for the last brook, and to be a Queen! How grand it sounds!" A very few steps brought her to the edge of the brook. "The Eighth Square at last!" she cried as she bounded across,

* * * * * *
 * * * * *
* * * * * *

and threw herself down to rest on a lawn as soft as moss, with little flower-beds dotted about it here and there. "Oh, how glad I am to get here! And what *is* this on my head?" she exclaimed in a tone of dismay, as she put her hands up to something very heavy that fitted tight all round her head.

"But how *can* it have got there without my knowing it?" she said to herself as she lifted it off and set it on her lap to make out what it could possibly be.

It was a golden crown.

L∞KING GLASS

QUEEN ALICE

"WELL, this *is* grand!" said Alice. "I never expected I should be a Queen so soon—and I'll tell you what it is, your Majesty," she went on, in a severe tone (she was always rather fond of scolding herself), "it'll never do for you to be lolling about on the grass like that! Queens have to be dignified, you know!"

So she got up and walked about—rather stiffly just at first, as she was afraid that the crown might come off; but she comforted herself with the thought that there was nobody to see her, "and if I really am a Queen," she said as she sat down again, "I shall be able to manage it quite well in time."

Everything was happening so oddly that she didn't feel a bit surprised at finding the Red Queen and the White Queen sitting close to her, one on each side. She would have liked

very much to ask them how they came there, but she feared it would not be quite civil. However, there would be no harm, she thought, in asking if the game was over. "Please, would you tell me—" she began, looking timidly at the Red Queen.

"Speak when you're spoken to!" the Queen sharply interrupted her.

"But if everybody obeyed that rule," said Alice, who was always ready for a little argument, "and if you only spoke when you were spoken to, and the other person always waited for *you* to begin, you see nobody would ever say anything, so that——"

"Ridiculous!" cried the Queen. "Why, don't you see, child—" here she broke off with a frown, and after thinking for a minute, suddenly changed the subject of the conversation. "What do you mean by 'If you really are a Queen'? What right have you to call yourself so? You can't be a Queen, you know, till you've passed the proper examination. And the sooner we begin it, the better."

[154]

# LOOKING GLASS

"I only said 'if'!" poor Alice pleaded in a piteous tone.

The two Queens looked at each other, and the Red Queen remarked, with a little shudder, "She *says* she only said 'if'——"

"But she said a great deal more than that!" the White Queen moaned, wringing her hands. "Oh, ever so much more than that!"

"So you did, you know," the Red Queen said to Alice. "Always speak the truth—think before you speak—and write it down afterwards."

"I'm sure I didn't mean—" Alice was beginning, but the Red Queen interrupted her impatiently.

"That's just what I complain of! You *should* have meant! What do you suppose is the use of a child without any meaning? Even a joke should have some meaning—and a child's more important than a joke, I hope. You couldn't deny that, even if you tried with both hands."

"I don't deny things with my *hands*," Alice objected.

"Nobody said you did," said the Red Queen. "I said you couldn't if you tried."

"She's in that state of mind," said the White Queen, "that she wants to deny *something*— only she doesn't know what to deny!"

"A nasty, vicious temper," the Red Queen remarked; and then there was an uncomfortable silence for a minute or two.

The Red Queen broke the silence by saying to the White Queen, "I invite you to Alice's dinner-party this afternoon."

The White Queen smiled feebly and said, "And I invite *you*."

"I didn't know I was to have a party at all," said Alice; "but if there *is* to be one, I think *I* ought to invite the guests."

"We gave you the opportunity of doing it," the Red Queen remarked; "but I daresay you've not had many lessons in manners yet?"

"Manners are not taught in lessons," said

It was a golden crown.

Page 152

And then all sorts of things happened.

Page 176

Alice. "Lessons teach you to do sums and things of that sort."

"Can you do Addition?" the White Queen asked. "What's one and one and one and one and one and one and one and one and one and one?"

"I don't know," said Alice. "I lost count."

"She can't do Addition," the Red Queen interrupted. "Can you do Subtraction? Take nine from eight."

"Nine from eight I can't, you know," Alice replied very readily; "but——"

"She can't do Subtraction," said the White Queen. "Can you do Division? Divide a loaf by a knife—what's the answer to *that*?"

"I suppose—" Alice was beginning, but the Red Queen answered for her. "Bread-and-butter, of course. Try another Subtraction sum. Take a bone from a dog; what remains?"

Alice considered. "The bone wouldn't remain, of course, if I took it, and the dog wouldn't remain; it would come to bite me—and I'm sure *I* shouldn't remain!"

"Then you think nothing would remain?" said the Red Queen.

"I think that's the answer."

"Wrong, as usual," said the Red Queen; "the dog's temper would remain."

"But I don't see how——"

"Why, look here!" the Red Queen cried. "The dog would lose its temper, wouldn't it?"

"Perhaps it would," Alice replied cautiously.

"Then if the dog went away, its temper would remain!" the Queen exclaimed triumphantly.

Alice said as gravely as she could, "They might go different ways." But she couldn't help thinking to herself, "What dreadful nonsense we *are* talking!"

"She can't do sums a *bit!*" the Queens said together with great emphasis.

"Can *you* do sums?" Alice said, turning suddenly on the White Queen, for she didn't like being found fault with so much.

The Queen gasped and shut her eyes. "I can do Addition," she said, "if you give me time," but I can't do Subtraction under *any* circumstances!"

"Of course you know your A B C?" said the Red Queen.

"To be sure I do," said Alice.

"So do I," the White Queen whispered; "we'll often say it over together, dear. And I'll tell you a secret—I can read words of one letter! Isn't *that* grand? However, don't be discouraged. You'll come to it in time."

Here the Red Queen began again. "Can you answer useful questions?" she said. "How is bread made?"

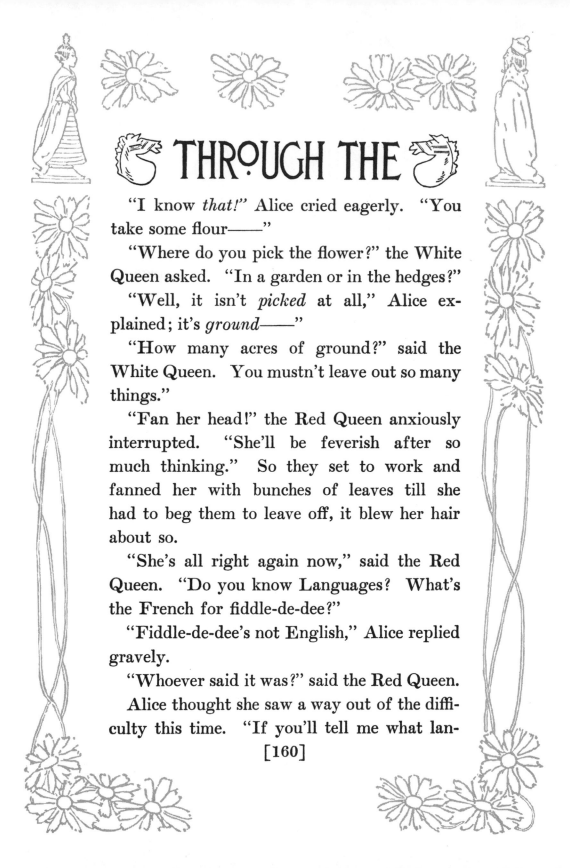

"I know *that!*" Alice cried eagerly. "You take some flour——"

"Where do you pick the flower?" the White Queen asked. "In a garden or in the hedges?"

"Well, it isn't *picked* at all," Alice explained; it's *ground*——"

"How many acres of ground?" said the White Queen. You mustn't leave out so many things."

"Fan her head!" the Red Queen anxiously interrupted. "She'll be feverish after so much thinking." So they set to work and fanned her with bunches of leaves till she had to beg them to leave off, it blew her hair about so.

"She's all right again now," said the Red Queen. "Do you know Languages? What's the French for fiddle-de-dee?"

"Fiddle-de-dee's not English," Alice replied gravely.

"Whoever said it was?" said the Red Queen.

Alice thought she saw a way out of the difficulty this time. "If you'll tell me what lan-

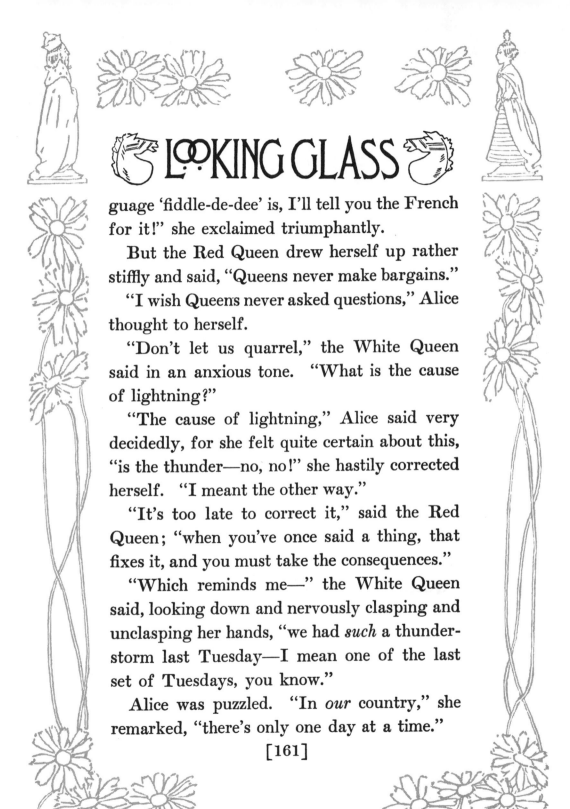

L♦♦KING GLASS

guage 'fiddle-de-dee' is, I'll tell you the French for it!" she exclaimed triumphantly.

But the Red Queen drew herself up rather stiffly and said, "Queens never make bargains."

"I wish Queens never asked questions," Alice thought to herself.

"Don't let us quarrel," the White Queen said in an anxious tone. "What is the cause of lightning?"

"The cause of lightning," Alice said very decidedly, for she felt quite certain about this, "is the thunder—no, no!" she hastily corrected herself. "I meant the other way."

"It's too late to correct it," said the Red Queen; "when you've once said a thing, that fixes it, and you must take the consequences."

"Which reminds me—" the White Queen said, looking down and nervously clasping and unclasping her hands, "we had *such* a thunderstorm last Tuesday—I mean one of the last set of Tuesdays, you know."

Alice was puzzled. "In *our* country," she remarked, "there's only one day at a time."

[161]

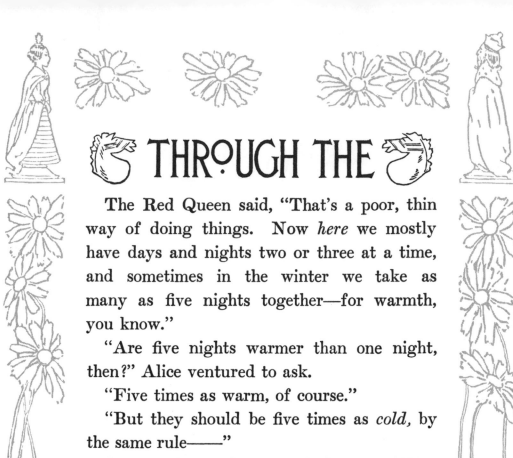

THROUGH THE

The Red Queen said, "That's a poor, thin way of doing things. Now *here* we mostly have days and nights two or three at a time, and sometimes in the winter we take as many as five nights together—for warmth, you know."

"Are five nights warmer than one night, then?" Alice ventured to ask.

"Five times as warm, of course."

"But they should be five times as *cold,* by the same rule——"

"Just so!" cried the Red Queen. "Five times as warm, *and* five times as cold—just as I'm five times as rich as you are, *and* five times as clever!"

Alice sighed and gave it up. "It's exactly like a riddle with no answer!" she thought.

"Humpty Dumpty saw it, too," the White Queen went on in a low voice, more as if she were talking to herself. "He came to the door with a corkscrew in his hand——"

"What did he want?" said the Red Queen.

"He said he *would* come in," the White

LOOKING GLASS

Queen went on, "because he was looking for a hippopotamus. Now, as it happened, there wasn't such a thing in the house that morning."

"Is there generally?" Alice asked in an astonished tone.

"Well, only on Thursdays," said the Queen.

"I know what he came for," said Alice; "he wanted to punish the fish, because——"

Here the White Queen began again. "It was *such* a thunderstorm, you can't think!" ("She *never* could, you know," said the Red Queen.) "And part of the roof came off, and ever so much thunder got in—and it went rolling round the room in great lumps—and knocking over the tables and things—till I was so frightened I couldn't remember my own name!"

Alice thought to herself, "I never should *try* to remember my name in the middle of an accident! Where would be the use of it?" but she did not say this aloud, for fear of hurting the poor Queen's feelings.

[163]

"Your Majesty must excuse her," the Red Queen said to Alice, taking one of the White Queen's hands in her own, and gently stroking it; "she means well, but she can't help saying foolish things as a general rule."

The White Queen looked timidly at Alice, who felt she *ought* to say something kind, but really couldn't think of anything at the moment.

"She never was really well brought up," the Red Queen went on; "but it's amazing how good-tempered she is! Pat her on the head and see how pleased she'll be!" But this was more than Alice had courage to do.

"A little kindness—and putting her hair in papers—would do wonders with her——"

The White Queen gave a deep sigh and laid her head on Alice's shoulder. "I *am* so sleepy!" she moaned.

"She's tired, poor thing!" said the Red Queen. "Smooth her hair, lend her your night-cap and sing her a soothing lullaby."

"I haven't got a nightcap with me," said

[164]

LOOKING GLASS

Alice, as she tried to obey the first direction, "and I don't know any soothing lullabies."

"I must do it myself, then," said the Red Queen, and she began:

"Hush-a-by, lady, in Alice's lap!
Till the feast's ready, we've time for a nap.
When the feast's over, we'll go to the ball—
Red Queen, and White Queen, and Alice, and all!"

"And now you know the words," she added, as she put her head down on Alice's other shoulder, "just sing it through to *me*. I'm getting sleepy, too." In another moment both Queens were fast asleep and snoring loud.

"What *am* I to do?" exclaimed Alice, looking about in great perplexity, as first one round head and then the other rolled down from her shoulder and lay like a heavy lump in her lap. "I don't think it *ever* happened before that any one had to take care of two Queens asleep at once! No, not in all the History of England— it couldn't, you know, because there never was more than one Queen at a time. Do wake up, you heavy things!" she went on in an impatient

tone; but there was no answer but a gentle
snoring.

The snoring got more distinct every minute,
and sounded more like a tune; at last she could
even make out words, and she listened so
eagerly that when the two great heads suddenly vanished from her lap she hardly missed
them.

She was standing before an arched doorway,
over which were the words "QUEEN
ALICE" in large letters, and on each side of
the arch there was a bell-handle; one was
marked "Visitors' Bell" and the other "Servants' Bell."

"I'll wait till the song's over," thought Alice,
"and then I'll ring the—the—*which* bell must
I ring?" she went on, very much puzzled by the
names. "I'm not a visitor and I'm not a servant. There *ought* to be one marked 'Queen,'
you know——"

Just then the door opened a little way and
a creature with a long beak put its head out
for a moment and said, "No admittance till the

LOOKING GLASS

week after next!" and shut the door again with a bang.

Alice knocked and rang in vain for a long time; but at last a very old Frog, who was sitting under a tree, got up and hobbled slowly toward her; he was dressed in bright yellow and had enormous boots on.

"What is it now?" the Frog said in a deep, hoarse whisper.

Alice turned round, ready to find fault with anybody. "Where's the servant whose business it is to answer the door?" she began angrily.

"Which door?" said the Frog.

Alice almost stamped with irritation at the slow drawl in which he spoke. *"This* door, of course!"

The Frog looked at the door with his large dull eyes for a minute; then he went nearer and rubbed it with his thumb, as if he were trying whether the paint would come off; then he looked at Alice.

"To answer the door?" he said. "What's

it been asking of?" He was so hoarse that Alice could scarcely hear him.

"I don't know what you mean," she said.

"I speaks English, doesn't I?" the Frog went on. "Or are you deaf? What did it ask you?"

"Nothing!" Alice said impatiently. "I've been knocking at it!"

"Shouldn't do that—shouldn't do that—" the Frog muttered. "Wexes it, you know." Then he went up and gave the door a kick with one of his great feet. "You let *it* alone," he panted out, as he hobbled back to his tree, "and it'll let *you* alone, you know."

At this moment the door was flung open and a shrill voice was heard singing:

*"To the Looking-Glass world it was Alice that said
'I've a sceptre in hand, I've a crown on my head.
Let the Looking-Glass creatures, whatever they be
Come and dine with the Red Queen, the White Queen,
and me!'"*

And hundreds of voices joined in the chorus:

 LOOKING GLASS

"Then fill up the glasses as quick as you can,
And sprinkle the table with buttons and bran:
Put cats in the coffee, and mice in the tea—
And welcome Queen Alice with thirty-times three!"

Then followed a confused noise of cheering, and Alice thought to herself, "Thirty times three makes ninety. I wonder if any one's counting?" In a minute there was silence again and the same shrill voice sang another verse:

"'O Looking-Glass creatures,' quoth Alice, 'draw
near!
'Tis an honor to see me, a favor to hear:
'Tis a privilege high to have dinner and tea
Along with the Red Queen, the White Queen, and
me!'"

Then came the chorus again:

"Then fill up the glasses with treacle and ink,
Or anything else that is pleasant to drink:
Mix sand with the cider, and wool with the wine—
And welcome Queen Alice with ninety-times-nine!"

"Ninety times nine!" Alice repeated in de-

[169]

spair. "Oh, that'll never be done! I'd better go in at once—" and in she went, and there was a dead silence the moment she appeared.

Alice glanced nervously along the table as she walked up the large hall, and noticed that there were about fifty guests of all kinds: some were animals, some birds, and there were even a few flowers among them. "I'm glad they've come without waiting to be asked," she thought; "I should never have known who were the right people to invite!"

There were three chairs at the head of the table. The Red and White Queens had already taken two of them, but the middle one was empty. Alice sat down in it, rather uncomfortable at the silence, and longing for some one to speak.

At last the Red Queen began. "You've missed the soup and fish," she said. "Put on the joint!" And the waiters set a leg of mutton before Alice, who looked at it rather anxiously, as she had never had to carve a joint before.

LOOKING GLASS

"You look a little shy; let me introduce you to that leg of mutton," said the Red Queen. "Alice—Mutton. Mutton—Alice." The leg of mutton got up in the dish and made a little bow to Alice, and Alice returned the bow, not knowing whether to be frightened or amused.

"May I give you a slice?" she said, taking up the knife and fork and looking from one Queen to the other.

"Certainly not," the Red Queen said, very decidedly; "it isn't etiquette to cut any one you've been introduced to. Remove the joint!" And the waiters carried it off and brought a large plum-pudding in its place.

"I won't be introduced to the pudding,

[171]

please," Alice said rather hastily, "or we shall get no dinner at all. May I give you some?"

But the Red Queen looked sulky and growled, "Pudding—Alice. Alice—Pudding. Remove the pudding!" and the waiters took it away so quickly that Alice couldn't return its bow.

However, she didn't see why the Red Queen should be the only one to give orders; so, as an experiment, she called out, "Waiter! Bring back the pudding!" and there it was again in a moment, like a conjuring-trick. It was so large that she couldn't help feeling a *little* shy with it, as she had been with the mutton; however, she conquered her shyness by a great effort and cut a slice and handed it to the Red Queen.

"What impertinence!" said the Pudding. "I wonder how you'd like it if I were to cut a slice out of *you*, you creature!"

It spoke in a thick, suety sort of voice, and Alice hadn't a word to say in reply; she could only sit and look at it and gasp.

[172]

L∞KING GLASS

"Make a remark," said the Red Queen; "it's ridiculous to leave all the conversation to the pudding!"

"Do you know, I've had such a quantity of poetry repeated to me to-day," Alice began, a little frightened at finding that the moment she opened her lips there was dead silence and all eyes were fixed upon her; "and it's a very curious thing, I think—every poem was about fishes in some way. Do you know why they're so fond of fishes all about here?"

She spoke to the Red Queen, whose answer was a little wide of the mark. "As to fishes," she said very slowly and solemnly, putting her mouth close to Alice's ear, "her White Majesty knows a lovely riddle—all in poetry—all about fishes. Shall she repeat it?"

"Her Red Majesty's very kind to mention it," the White Queen murmured into Alice's other ear in a voice like the cooing of a pigeon. "It would be *such* a treat! May I?"

"Please do," Alice said very politely.

THROUGH THE

The White Queen laughed with delight and stroked Alice's cheek. Then she began:

" *'First, the fish must be caught.'*
That is easy: a baby, I think, could have caught it.
'Next, the fish must be bought.'
That is easy: a penny, I think, would have bought it.

" *'Now cook me the fish!'*
That is easy, and will not take more than a minute.
'Let it lie in a dish!'
That is easy, because it already is in it.

" *'Bring it here! Let me sup!'*
It is easy to set such a dish on the table.
'Take the dish-cover up!'
Ah, that is so hard that I fear I'm unable!

" *'For it holds it like glue—*
Holds the lid to the dish, while it lies in the middle:
Which is easiest to do,
Un-dish-cover the fish, or dishcover the riddle?' "

"Take a minute to think about it, and then guess," said the Red Queen. "Meanwhile, we'll drink your health—Queen Alice's health!" she screamed at the top of her voice, and all the

[174]

# LOOKING GLASS

guests began drinking it directly, and very queerly they managed it: some of them put their glasses upon their heads like extinguishers and drank all that trickled down their faces; others upset the decanters and drank the wine as it ran off the edges of the table; and three of them (who looked like kangaroos) scrambled into the dish of roast mutton and began eagerly lapping up the gravy, "just like pigs in a trough!" thought Alice.

"You ought to return thanks in a neat speech," the Red Queen said, frowning at Alice as she spoke.

"We must support you, you know," the White Queen whispered, as Alice got up to do it, very obediently, but a little frightened.

"Thank you very much," she whispered in reply, "but I can do quite well without."

"That wouldn't be at all the thing," the Red Queen said very decidedly; so Alice tried to submit to it with a good grace.

("And they *did* push so!" she said afterwards when she was telling her sister the his-

tory of the feast. "You would have thought they wanted to squeeze me flat!")

In fact, it was rather difficult for her to keep in her place while she made her speech; the two Queens pushed her so, one on each side, that they nearly lifted her up into the air. "I rise to return thanks—" Alice began, and she really *did* rise as she spoke several inches; but she got hold of the edge of the table and managed to pull herself down again.

"Take care of yourself!" screamed the White Queen, seizing Alice's hair with both her hands. "Something's going to happen!"

And then (as Alice afterwards described it) all sorts of things happened in a moment. The candles all grew up to the ceiling, looking something like a bed of rushes with fireworks at the top. As to the bottles, they each took a pair of plates, which they hastily fitted on as wings, and so, with forks for legs, went fluttering about in all directions; "and very like birds they look," Alice thought to herself as well as

[176]

she could in the dreadful confusion that was beginning.

At this moment she heard a hoarse laugh at her side, and turned to see what was the matter with the White Queen; but instead of the Queen, there was the leg of mutton sitting in the chair. "Here I am!" cried a voice from the soup-tureen, and Alice turned again just in time to see the Queen's broad, good-natured face grinning at her for a moment over the edge of the tureen before she disappeared into the soup.

There was not a moment to be lost. Already several of the guests were lying down in the dishes, and the soup-ladle was walking up the table towards Alice's chair and beckoning to her impatiently to get out of its way.

"I can't stand this any longer!" she cried, as she jumped up and seized the tablecloth with both hands. One good pull, and plates, dishes, guests and candles came crashing down together in a heap on the floor.

"And as for *you*," she went on, turning

 THROUGH THE

fiercely upon the Red Queen, whom she considered as the cause of all the mischief—but the Queen was no longer at her side; she had suddenly dwindled down to the size of a little doll and was now on the table, merrily running round and round after her own shawl, which was trailing behind her.

At any other time Alice would have felt surprised at this, but she was far too much excited to be surprised at anything *now*. "As for *you*," she repeated, catching hold of the little creature in the very act of jumping over a bottle which had just lighted upon the table, "I'll shake you into a kitten, that I will!"

LOOKING GLASS

SHAKING

SHE took her off the table as she spoke and shook her backwards and forwards with all her might.

The Red Queen made no resistance whatever; only her face grew very small and her eyes got large and green; and still, as Alice went on shaking her, she kept on growing shorter—and fatter—and softer—and rounder—and——

THROUGH THE

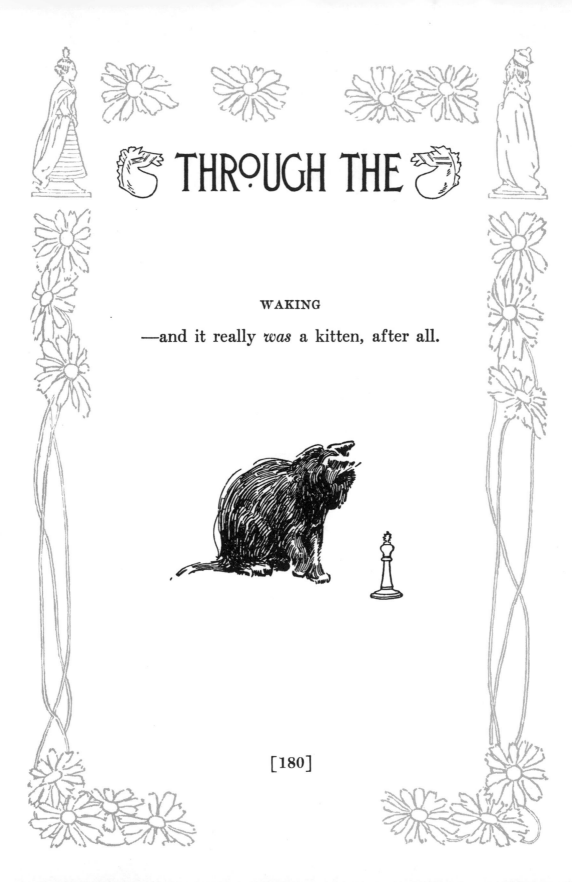

WAKING

—and it really *was* a kitten, after all.

LOOKING GLASS

WHICH DREAMED IT?

"**Y**OUR Red Majesty shouldn't purr so loud," Alice said, rubbing her eyes and addressing the kitten respectfully, yet with some severity. "You woke me out of oh! such a nice dream! And you've been along with me, Kitty—all through the Looking-Glass world. Did you know it, dear?"

It is a very inconvenient habit of kittens (Alice had once made the remark) that whatever you say to them they *always* purr. "If they would only purr for 'yes' and mew for 'no,' or any rule of that sort," she had said, "so that one could keep up a conversation! But how *can* you talk with a person if they *always* say the same thing?"

On this occasion the kitten only purred, and it was impossible to guess whether it meant "yes" or "no."

[181]

 # THROUGH THE

So Alice hunted among the chessmen on the table till she had found the Red Queen; then she went down on her knees on the hearth-rug and put the kitten and the Queen to look at each other. "Now, Kitty," she cried, clapping her hands triumphantly, "confess that was what you turned into!"

("But it wouldn't look at it," she said when she was explaining the thing afterwards to her sister; "it turned away its head and pretended not to see it; but it looked a *little* ashamed of itself, so I think it *must* have been the Red Queen.")

"Sit up a little more stiffly, dear!" Alice cried with a merry laugh. "And curtsey while you're thinking what to—what to purr. It saves time, remember!" And she caught it up and gave it one little kiss, "just in honor of its having been a Red Queen."

"Snowdrop, my pet!" she went on, looking over her shoulder at the White Kitten, which was still patiently undergoing its toilet, "when *will* Dinah have finished with your White

LOOKING GLASS

Majesty, I wonder? That must be the reason you were so untidy in my dream. Dinah! Do you know that you're scrubbing a White Queen? Really, it's most disrespectful of you!

"And what did *Dinah* turn to, I wonder?" she prattled on, as she settled comfortably down with one elbow on the rug and her chin in her hand, to watch the kittens. "Tell me, Dinah, did you turn to Humpty Dumpty? I *think* you did; however, you'd better not mention it to your friends just yet, for I'm not sure.

"By the way, Kitty, if only you'd been really with me in my dream, there was one thing you *would* have enjoyed—I had such a quantity of poetry said to me, all about fishes! To-morrow morning you shall have a real treat. All the time you're eating your breakfast I'll repeat 'The Walrus and the Carpenter' to you, and then you can make believe it's oysters, dear!

"Now, Kitty, let's consider who it was that dreamed it all. This is a serious question, my

THROUGH THE

dear, and you should *not* go on licking your paw like that—as if Dinah hadn't washed you this morning! You see, Kitty, it *must* have been either me or the Red King. He was part of my dream, of course—but then I was part of his dream, too! *Was* it the Red King, Kitty? You were his wife, my dear, so you ought to know. Oh, Kitty, *do* help to settle it! I'm sure your paw can wait!" But the provoking kitten only began on the other paw and pretended it hadn't heard the question.

Which do *you* think it was?

A BOAT, beneath a sunny sky
Lingering onward dreamily
In an evening of July—

Children three that nestle near,
Eager eye and willing ear,
Pleased a simple tale to hear—

Long has paled that sunny sky:
Echoes fade and memories die:
Autumn frosts have slain July.

[184]

LOOKING GLASS

Still she haunts me, phantomwise,
Alice moving under skies
Never seen by waking eyes.

Children yet, the tale to hear,
Eager eye and willing ear,
Lovingly shall nestle near.

In a Wonderland they lie,
Dreaming as the days go by,
Dreaming as the summers die:

Ever drifting down the stream—
Lingering in the golden gleam—
Life, what is it but a dream?

THE END

[185]

CHRISTMAS-GREETINGS

[FROM A FAIRY TO A CHILD]

LADY dear, if Fairies may
    For a moment lay aside
Cunning tricks and elfish play,
    'Tis at happy Christmas-tide.

We have heard the children say—
    Gentle children, whom we love—
Long ago, on Christmas Day,
    Came a message from above.

Still, as Christmas-tide comes round,
    They remember it again—
Echo still the joyful sound
    "Peace on earth, good-will to men!"

Yet the hearts must childlike be
    Where such heavenly guests abide;
Unto children, in their glee,
    All the year is Christmas-tide!

Thus, forgetting tricks and play
    For a moment, Lady dear,
We would wish you, if we may,
    Merry Christmas, glad New Year!

Christmas, 1867.

[186]